THE FIGHT
FOR
SPACE

THE FIGHT FOR SPACE

Roberto Ontiveros

STEPHEN F. AUSTIN STATE UNIVERSITY PRESS

The pieces in this collection have appeared in the following publications:

"Plans in Construction Paper," *The Threepenny Review,* Fall 2003

"Phoenix Framing," *Beloit Fiction Journal,* Spring 2004

"The Fight for Space," *Santa Monica Review,* Spring 2005

"They Let Me Drive," *The Threepenny Review,* Spring 2006

Hecho en Tejas (University of New Mexico Press), 2007

"The Love You Belt," *Santa Monica Review,* Spring 2006

"Ruby Coast," *Santa Monica Review,* Spring 2007

"Open House," *Santa Monica Review,* Spring 2008

"The Applications," *The Threepenny Review,* Summer 2009

"Curfew," *Santa Monica Review,* Spring 2012

"The Offices of Fang and Claw," *Santa Monica Review,* Spring 2014

"Red Lines Drawn in the Blue Room," *Huizache,* Spring 2017

CONTENTS

Plans in Construction Paper

Beverly was pacing outside the café, *almost* walking in for ten minutes, scooting her feet over loose gravel and discarded cigarette butts. She was talking on a cell phone in the patio area, looking mad and crazy, leaning on somebody's parked mini-van, then walking over to the plastic trash bin, softly kicking its green plastic skin. From the booth by the window where I sat and stirred sugar into my coffee, Beverly looked as if she were arguing with a lover she could never give up, then as if she were trying to offer directions to a TV deliveryman. Her made-up face was busy with serious movement, lips, and brow getting diplomatic, then abandoning their quick wrinkle of diplomacy and becoming stern. Last year, when Beverly and I were dating, when I had a steady occupation and a life plan, watching her on the phone like that would have killed me. In league with the anxious and wounded sect of men who want to keep their jobs, their girlfriends, their quiet places in town, I felt threatened whenever I saw anyone seeking a public privacy. In weakness, I could not watch office jokers snickering by a water cooler. I would feel a shift in my gut when it looked as if some brave soul was getting ready to ask an unsuspecting spirit out on a date. Now, I am cool with everything; I know that. And I don't need a showered and powdered throng of clock-ins who, through the inconveniences of nine-to-five pleasantries, are obliged to shoot off inane platitudes or hide from the boss. With no job, no girlfriend, and no place in the city, I have become serene. I can meet Beverly for coffee and have an actual conversation and not be blown into hysterics by the caffeine. I can watch her yap on her cell phone and not be under the politics of the muffled head noises that used to surround and fence my every stratagem.

Beverly stopped by my apartment earlier that day. I was in the shower, and she called out to me as I scrubbed the suds of shampoo from my neck and shoulders: "Hey, Terry, I know we had plans to meet at five, and that's still on, but I was walking past your place and thought I'd come in. See what you were up to." I hollered back a hello but did not speed up my shower just to accommodate a girl who lacked the social sense to walk away from a door when a knock is not answered. Besides, when I got out of the shower, Beverly was gone. There was a note pinned to my fridge, reminding me of our date. Beverly and I had not spoken, I mean *really* spoken (talked about our lusts and limits and the ways we had let our respective worldviews slide) in over a year. And I had given up even thinking about our good times, about the Art Brut gallery we once walked through and the Rossellini movies we watched when we weren't publicly dating. Beverly and I used to go out at least three times a week, and we felt like a sexy couple; we screamed inappropriate insults at each other and found our definitive calm whenever we were apart. We were not good for each other. I did not believe that Beverly needed closure. And I knew that I did not. We had bumped into each other at the mall and grocery store; there were no mean faces, and there was zero attraction. We could wish each other well, and so we did. Out of nowhere on a Friday morning, she called and wanted to meet and talk. I started to approach a kind of discomfort and anger I had not felt in over a year, and I asked her outright what she wanted to talk about.

"I'm leaving town. And I want to say my goodbyes."

"Goodbyes?"

"Yes. You aren't the only person I'm calling."

"Yeah, just the first, right?"

"No, not the first."

We got quiet; enough time for me to feel like an idiot and understand that Beverly owed me nothing, and that was a state I had tried to encourage. More, I knew I would, in all honesty, get a kick out of seeing her, especially if she was leaving town.

Right out of the shower, once I had called her name and realized she had left, I sat on the couch, drying chest and shoulders with a towel and looking around the room where Beverly had just been. I got up and walked to the kitchen. There was a glass in the otherwise empty sink and a drip from the faucet. I guessed I could trust her walking-through-the-neighborhood story and assume that she needed hydration. I got up to shut off the faucet and saw a notebook that wasn't mine; it was a leather-bound address organizer that looked as if it had been passed from angst-ridden teenager to angst-ridden twenty-something for over a decade. Haphazardly, I grabbed it, and a sheet of yellow construction paper slid out and caught its showy glide to the linoleum. Not bothering with the sheet, I opened up the book and found—besides about thirty loose sheets of construction paper, mostly yellow, but there was also blue and baby blue—a recent photograph of Beverly.

To my surprise, I found myself gripping the notebook with the kind of jolt and sudden knuckle tension that sent a few more sheets of construction paper on their graceful dive. Beverly had cut her hair. Short and sexy, chocolate tresses hung suspended in blow-dried curls over her white shoulders. She was not smiling, but I knew that look, with her left eyebrow deciding whether it should raise a question, her eyes widening to emphasize mock worry. Beverly was happy. In this picture, Beverly looked glad to be alive. I put it down where she had left it and got ready for our date. I wanted to dress up nice for her, let her think I was moderately prosperous and functioning, but the pinstriped pants I wanted to wear felt tight, and all the button-up shirts that would have matched them were dirty anyway. I threw on a pair of blue jeans and a black T-shirt and went back to look at the notebook. The appointment pages were inked with dates and errands to run. *Go see Dr. Ruiz about selling your car. Check out the hostel situation in Canada. See about language schools in Chile. Get a passport.*

Beverly was in action, and that was okay, but what struck me as strange was that on each sheet of construction paper, written with a felt-tip marker, there was a statement about her future. Each statement was mutually exclusive. *You are thirty years old and watering a lawn in Abilene, TX. You are thirty years old and walking up the steps of the Cologne Cathedral. You are thirty and avoiding pregnancy in Puerto Rico.* It was like some terrible joke about chance. Beverly was twenty-six, and this kind of projection seemed outside of her character and too personal for me to be looking at. When it was time to go, I made sure to bring the notebook with me. Beverly had spent private energy on it, and I did not want to be responsible for its loss. Once at the café, I decided to leave the notebook in the car until she asked for it. If I brought it in, that would have been all we talked about.

When Beverly decided to get off the phone and start our date, she immediately ran over to scoot herself in the booth seat across from me. She must have seen me through the window. I started rising to give her a hug or kiss her on the cheek, but she was already planted, and now she was clasping my hands and saying how good it was to see me. Her palms and fingers were so warm I could feel sweat start up in my own, and I slowly eased out of her grip before she let go. She was going to say something that would freak me out. I just knew it. She was going to drop a subpoena on me, say I owed her money, or tell me she got a job at an antique store and now needs back the jewelry boxes she left at my apartment. So, I chimed in, "God, Beverly, you look terrific!" Maybe she did. It was too fast for me to find arousal or even contentment in her looks. She was dressed as if she cared what people thought about her: skirt and blouse and everything ironed, earrings that seemed to match her flats and the watery joy in her brown eyes.

She exhaled with sentiment and consideration, and then said, "I feel terrific. I feel so..."—eyes looking up at the ceiling, then at me, she grabbed for my hands again—"I just feel so *much*, in general."

What the hell? Was she on something? Had Beverly just found Jesus or the Buddha within, or maybe she was getting married? No, I remembered, she was leaving town. "So, where are you planning on escaping?"

"I'm not saying."

"I suppose that means no new mailing address."

"Terry, I'm not saying because I do not know."

Beverly explained to me how she had spent the last six months saving and borrowing enough money just to get away, to go anywhere for at least a summer, and she did not want to force a locality upon herself. Beverly was never good at saving money, always buying CDs and eating out every meal. If she had swung this caper, then she must be a very different person from the girl I cheated on and eventually was too ashamed to show my face around. I did not want to talk about where she might be traveling. And she did not want to talk about why. But I had seen what was written on those sheets of construction paper and had my hints. Beverly was always one to be defined by her company. When we were dating, I could measure how close we were by how little she threw in her opinion. It was not a characteristic I liked being around. Maybe she had come to deal with her acquiescent nature, and maybe she wanted to shake up her scene, drop her pliant roles, and be someone else for a while. Maybe that was her long-term goal. Why the hell not? The one thing that losing my "long term" ambition had taught me (besides how to appreciate the poetry of late-night TV and the quiet dignity in the people who deliver my mail) was how hollow an enterprise it was to think a new scene would burn away the deadness of a life. At least for me. I wanted somehow to spare Beverly that lesson because when that lesson hits you, the first thing you feel is shame. Before any serenity, you have to eat a lot of fear.

"Maybe if you stuck around we could start seeing each other again."

"You don't mean that. And you don't want that." She saved me the "neither do I" by slowly letting go of my hands and then calling a waitress over to order a chai tea. Beverly asked about my job situation, so I went in on it. I had quit the office, quit the comic book store, gotten fired from the moving company, and just stopped going to the tree-farming gig. Somehow, because I could always find quick work, I had enough to live and eat and drink, and—when I got my laundry and libido together—go out on a few dates. Life was life, and if it had ever been more, then I had perhaps been less. We talked for a little over an hour, and there was no judgment if there was also no love. I found out that while she had been outside the café on the cell phone, she was, in fact, putting the final break-up touches on a guy she had been seeing for a month. She had hoped to meet him for drinks after she met with me for coffee. The call did not go so well, and she was now without a ride.

"Lucky I brought my car."

"Oh, yeah, I'm *so* lucky."

I felt nervous when I realized the same Peter Gabriel tape was hanging out of the mouth of the stereo since the last night we went out. For sure I had listened to something else besides this tape, but maybe I hadn't, maybe I hadn't even played it all year.

We were at her door in five minutes, and there was not a moment when I thought we would kiss or give deep lung-crushing hugs. Beverly smiled. I repeated to her that I thought she looked terrific, which I now could concede was true. Then Beverly pulled her hand out to pinch my belly through the fabric of the worn T-shirt material.

"So do you, Terry. I always thought so, and I still do."

Then I remembered that her notebook was in the glove compartment. "Wait," I said and jogged back to the car. When Beverly saw what I pulled out of the door, her look of shock and relief was enough to make me want to beg her to stay in town, just so we could become friends again, rent movies together, gossip, tell jokes.

"You left this in my kitchen when you stopped by during your walk."

"Man, I didn't even know I had lost it." She seemed afraid. "Did you look through it?"

"Some papers fell out when I picked it off the counter. Don't worry; I put them back in."

Back at the apartment, I pulled off my shirt and went to the fridge to grab a beer. The first sheet of construction paper that had fallen out of her notebook was still on the kitchen floor. After I grabbed a can, I picked up the sheet and walked over to the couch. In the center of the yellow sheet of construction paper were the words: *I am thirty years old, sitting in an Italian movie theater, watching* Open City. There was a two-day-old newspaper by the remote control. I had spent the fifty cents to see what films were showing and to read the personals ads. I opened it up to the job section and found a travel agency that wanted a full-timer with some managerial experience. I wrote down the number to call on the sheet of construction paper that I was now using as a coaster for my beer, right over the word "thirty."

Phoenix Framing

I hate thinking about my job—*any* job, doesn't matter what kind—when I'm not on the clock, but since I'm getting fired tomorrow, I'm nursing this itch to slam myself. Phoenix Framing was already doing poor business when I put in an application, a doomed, desperate-looking place: flecks of olive paint peeling off the beige store sign, finger smears curling into the dust-caked glass door. I always felt guilty for not buying postcards and decals there. Church, the hippie burn-out who ran the print shop/gallery, was going through a divorce and getting trashed every night. The twenty bucks I lifted from the register were not going to trip up his nightlife routine. I would see him at The Bolo Lounge, sitting alone, slow sipping pints of Guinness, then slamming down a few tequila shots. Church was mixing up his booze, imbibing in an order that ensured the sickest possible morning. He was entirely too hungover to work the day shifts, so he needed to hire on some young blood. I was not so young, but having no degree and being into painting felt that this might be a perfect work situation. In my mind, I figured Church would let me show up around ten, drink coffee until noon, then eat a sandwich, and walk home.

My apartment sits four quiet blocks away from the commercial stretch of town in whichPhoenix is located, and is not so different from Church's shop. I have framed Klee and Ernst prints hung up along the hall that leads to the bathroom, and nine cheap *Nosferatu* postcards pinned to the fridge with alphabet magnets. The genuine differences between my place and the print store are all the empty beer bottles and dirty ashtrays. I do not smoke, but every girlfriend I ever have always does. Whenever they go, I freeze the place up for weeks, trying to learn from whatever litter was left, from whatever hair scrunchies and stray lipsticks I find in the medicine cabinet, the address books and gum wrappers tucked under couch cushions. I wanted to work at Phoenix because on the inside, it looked like a cleaned up version of my pad, plus there was no history for me in that climate controlled space, no spilled wine on the carpet, cigarette burns on the mini-blinds, and memories of bad love and worse conversation. Plus, I liked that a bum like Church could run a store. Church might have even been a painter, too, at one point. The Formica™ table in the back room was stacked with yellow legal pads, and from the pages of pen marks, it looked as if Church spent his talent drawing lower backs and ankles. I used to think that all the drawings meant Church was going over his idea of a dream girl, some fantasy chick whom he was trying to pencil down the best parts of in the snatches of time he seized between ordering supplies and mulling over the day's pitiable receipts. The more I looked at the stacks of scribbled pages, the more they began to resemble a study or even a meditation. None of the drawings were any good. If Church *was* an artist, then maybe lower bodies were the only forms he could not draw, and it had become his life's work to wrestle with the shadow tricks involved in detailing waist-down anatomy.

The legs Church drew were well-shaped, firm, and almost looked, in their unabashed thickness, like sexy animation: R. Crumb, Max Fleischer, or all that too-skinny Japanese Manga made heavy and so human. The loose charcoal lines and strict ballpoint etching gave the impression of a sudden death to what was once a fluid movement. Whatever these legs and haunches were supposed to trigger, all their charcoal vertices predominantly functioned as a showcase to a strain of violent stillness or end, and they looked as if they represented someone real, someone living. I knew that these could not be drawings of Church's wife; Sharon was stick-thin. Church kept a photo of her on his desk. Even though the two of them were separated, he never thought to put the photo face down or tuck it in a drawer. The girl in the picture was seventeen years younger than my boss, pretty in a way that reaches a point of maximum delicacy but might go mousy or bitter. Sharon, a girl two years my senior, was about twenty-three when they married. Church, a few months from fifty, was, I reasoned, a handsome man. His eyes were clear, had that mean kid glint; his shoulder-length black hair streaked silver at his temples, was thick as a Chow's mane, and was kept in a ponytail. He was a snappy dresser, too, no oversized Corona T-shirts and flip-flops, a real natural fiber guy. Church did not eat meat, but he wore leather: cowboy vests, rodeo belts, the basic rawhide filigree. My boss didn't think it was bad that I drank so much coffee or that I never wanted to smoke pot with him in the alley behind the shop when he came in to take over the register. I got along with Church in reassuring ways that made me feel bad for ever having bad thoughts about him, which I used to hold all the time. I have always lived in town, and Church was a welcomed regular at every café or coffee joint I frequented. As I teenager, I used to look at Church and feel the weirdest resentment. He was like this cool dad, cool uncle, accepted everywhere, and always being brought into a conversation. Everyone trusted him, and to me, that made him suspect.

A WEEK AFTER I started working for Church, I was drinking at the Bolo Lounge and saw my new boss's wife. She was very hot, but skinny—skinny like the kind of thing that makes you feel perverted for appreciating it. She had no tits and no ass, but it was hard not to find her sexy. Sharon was hanging out with another guy. The man looked like a less healthy, more broke example of Church. The two of them were playing pool, and she was laughing and laughing and sounded coked-up. I found myself feeling angry with her, but I didn't know if she had left Church or if he had left her or why I should have a stake in the matter. So, I grew steady, and after a few pints, went home.

Once in my apartment, I started to draw into a sketchbook that my last girlfriend, Meg, had left wedged under my mattress. Meg had wanted us to be (in anticipation of the creative yoke that would bind us) "art pals," to spend our evenings doing sketches and watercolor work, the both of us stretched out on the floor listening to Dead Can Dance or Tangerine Dream, faux-music I could only stomach if I was drunk or we were fucking. In the end, Meg never got any work done, and I felt as if the woman had smuggled large capacities for spontaneous joy out of me. Before drawing in Meg's tablet, I examined her work: a shrill succession of three-dimensional squares. Inside every panel, Meg had drawn a futuristic-looking shaven head, a comic strip with the same chemotherapy patient looking straight out in gangly focus, awaiting his phrenologist, deciding when to go ahead with the lobotomy. Meg's two favorite movies (*THX 1138* and *Fantastic Planet*) were both dystopian science fiction, and this quirk in cinema taste came across in her art. She had drawn three full pages in this manner; it spooked me, reminded me of the mystery I thought I found in her. I tore them out and stuck them farther into the last clean sheets in the back of the tablet, careful not to smudge her work even though if I ever ran into Meg again, we probably wouldn't speak. She definitely wouldn't want any of the drawings she had done while we were together.

I drew a bunch of arms and went to bed.

When I got to Phoenix the next day, Church had hung up a wall's worth of new pieces. He was good to the kids in town; he always let them show some of their work in his store. It wasn't ever that bad. When the high school art students knew they were going to have a piece on display, they would put everything into it, buy an appropriate frame, take time with the gesso and fixative, and be good about signing their names. It was nice to look at in the morning; all those newspaper collages and pastel works were safe on the retina, never any deeper than the joy of their effort or the splayed attention to learning a new technique. After I punched in my time card and counted the money in the register, I walked over to the wall of novice art and drank my coffee. They were seriously going over each separate work, smiling, happy with how vital each canvas and framed sheet of paper looked. *Yeah, this is how it should be*, I thought, *pure and preened of all affectations.* Then I saw the drawing of the leg: a rough looking gesture sketch, hasty black crayon marks on a single sheet of manila paper and framed in black metal. It was signed by Church and dated two weeks back. The price underneath the picture was $150. That was twelve bucks more than I was making a week.

What I didn't like about the drawing was that, on its own, *not* framed, but maybe lying on the floor or stuck in a notebook of private dream sketches, I knew the lines and daubs of ink that came together to create a calf or a knee were exactly as special as any of the dozens of self-indulgent sketches I used to churn out when I was living with Meg. It was an audience-weary effort that nevertheless wanted the opportunity to earn admirers. The picture wanted too much. I had, of course, drawn loony junk like that before, and my pieces were never any different: black wax pencil smears and bold ink streaks, little more than automatic scratch work, derivative of everything loose and uncensored and not worth framing. However, if I ever *did* frame one of these drawings, then the aesthetics would have to change. The abrupt attention that would be paid to the swift charcoal lines and finger rubbings would lend any of the pieces a fierce quality suggestive of romantic flight and the consequences of unchecked caprice.

I really loved seeing Church's picture on the wall. I have never had the balls to frame any of my rough work, no matter how much I enjoyed looking at them or how many people expressed to me that I had done a fine job experimenting.

At the Bolo Lounge, I decided that I wanted to talk to someone: a boozer with the shakes, a girl waiting for a friend, an energy drink representative, whoever, but there was no one. I was in the habit of showing up at the bar early in the evening, then leaving before the night picked up with hipster traffic. Bolo wasn't a dive, but it wasn't anywhere you'd take anyone you wanted to impress.

I was staying longer than I usually did and had started to draw on napkins, jotting out frenetic pen marks that crowned and froze-up, then went to knots and claws. This was my favorite activity and probably why I never got anywhere with my large canvas efforts. It was just so fulfilling to dick with these wee-scaled smear-works. There was nocturnal beauty and sleepy jazz in every one of my decorated napkins.

A tight crowd of after-hours office-types shuffled into the Bolo Lounge and sat at a table in the center of the place. Two women in leather skirts came in, looked around as if they were unsure about wanting to be where they suddenly were, as if they might leave, but after two minutes, they decided to sit on the swivel stools by the bar. I was crouched in the back corner of the place, a pen by my beer but no tablet. I gave up thinking that sitting in the corner of a cantina and drawing pictures ever looked cool after I saw other guys doing it. It doesn't matter how old you are. You can be fifteen, as old as Church, or older; it doesn't matter because you always look too old to be doing what you are doing. I liked drawing on napkins. The barmaids would never fail to pick them up when they came over to clear the table, and then I was done having to think that drawing ever meant anything. When this happened, I felt a lap of gratitude and would leave bigger tips if they didn't ask if it was okay to toss the napkins but just snatched them up as if there was never a question.

I stood to leave, but before I moved from the table, I stuffed the four napkins on which I had been scribbling into my back pocket.

The TV and VCR were on when I walked into my apartment. There was a lazy heat around the entertainment area. I had been sleeping in front of the monitor for weeks, and it was easier for me. Beds hold memories that color dreams, so I kept a pillow and afghan under the remote control. Coming home from Bolo, I just plopped down on my knees to watch the old gangster movie that had been rewinding and replaying since I left for work. A black and white face was kissing a black and white face. I felt cold, so I pulled the afghan over my lap, then onto my shoulders and, feeling safe, nodded off before the set. When I woke up four hours later, the clock on the VCR said it was 5:27. On screen, a black and white hand was reaching into a black and white pocket.

"WHAT HAPPENED BETWEEN YOU and Sharon?" I asked Church, puncturing twenty minutes of storefront silence, bugging him with a question that was none of my business and should have put me on his list of the tactless, irredeemable. "I mean, who left who?"

Church, who had been pacing the store space in a rising-sliding horseshoe pattern along the linoleum tiles, stopped, not so suddenly as to indicate that a personal line had been crossed. He looked my way, flashed a sore smile, then resumed his sauntering pace. After about twenty seconds, he said, "I dumped her for myself, for my sake."

"Oh, yeah."

"I don't mean that I was in an—what do they like to say, *abusive?* Yeah, abusive relationship. No, we got along fine. I dumped Sharon so that I could go healthy. Be clean, you know."

"Bullshit, man, you booze as much as I do. Also, you're older. You aren't healthy."

"Yeah, I booze," Church said, then got quiet for a pull before adding, "I was unfaithful to Sharon. She deserved to get out while she was still pretty for the world. We didn't argue when I told her that we were done. She knew the breakup was coming. We kissed, hugged, and then I drove her back to her parents. She even came over two days later, and we packed up her clothes and books into cardboard boxes together. In harmony. In respect."

"Man," I said, starting to grin and wanting to tease Church. "So, you dirt fiend, who did you dump her for?"

He stopped again; his shoulders stiffened. This might have been the part he never wanted to have to explain, but Church seemed to be in a gut-spilling mood. "There wasn't another girl. I was cheating on Sharon, in a sense, with myself."

And that didn't mean that he was locked away in a room, looking at childhood photographs or rereading all his old diaries.

 Church (slow but willing to inform me) was no longer able to speak to most people without feeling crowded or mashed or caged. "It's not as if my mind is filled with too much noise or color or any unwarranted jazz. It's more like I can't see why I should speak to anyone anymore. Forget about me getting into any other relationship. This past week has been quiet and healing. You and I can talk because I know that you are in no way seriously bound to me. I mean, you work for me, and money is exchanged, but we're in no danger of being total pals, so I can tell you. I feel as if I have undergone a kind of surgery and, who knows, maybe I've had a tiny stroke. I go to bars by myself, sit and drink, and feel like I have found a new girlfriend."

I DIDN'T WANT TO be a painter. Not even the invisible, no-profit painter that I already was. I knew that for me, art would make real life of pungent self-tolerance. It was easier for Church to get away with this kind of sticky confidence and attachment. Church ran a shop that provided local gallery service. Church had a hot wife that he wasn't seeing anymore, out of respect for her pride and well-being. Church was drinking a lot but being a cool guy, being nice, buying cab rides for anyone too trashed to drive or walk home from Bolo Lounge. I was just drinking a lot. All beer. I was off the hard stuff. On good nights, it was ten cans; on the nights when I didn't hold back, I could binge on a case of eighteen—no joke—twelve if they were tall-boys. I was grateful when it was just over a six-pack, but I drank every night, a couple of beers at Bolo Lounge and then whatever I had in the fridge at home. I wasn't getting anything out of it except a slow buzz that took two hours to obtain and a friendly, cozy blanket high, which is, I guess, what everyone at this stage of rising or shrinking alcoholism gets out of drinking.

I was trying to do the same with painting. There was no way I was going to just quit with all the paint and paper and sheets of canvas lying around. I had put down real cash for these materials, and it wasn't as if I didn't have any art in me. I still wanted to draw and scratch epiphany-glyphs across the paper, spit on a canvas and rub a crumb of charcoal into the white surface. I still had the desire, but my supplies were dwindling. When they were gone, I wasn't going to purchase anymore. I had already used up my oil pastels and colored chalk, and since I ran out of black paint, which was the non-color I got the most from, I was more or less out of everything, but I kept working. I wanted to end the farce, spend my supplies, and be done with it all. Earlier that week, I was engaged in these horrible pointillist mandalas, sharp rose and sallow flesh-hued stabs circling each other's pigment on torn planks of cardboard. Then I was out of cardboard and, searching the room for something more, found a set of paper plates still in their plastic shrink-wrap. When I was done scissoring them into little squares, I dipped my fingers into a bottle of black ink and thumbed crude cochlea swirls onto the cheap white.

There were all these extra bits of paper plate, too small to paint or draw on, but I could place them next to each other, set them on a flat surface, and make a blanche collage. I had this poster-sized square of thin plywood off of which I'd been eating my dinner, even though it was just splintering wood, legless and ugly. I'd always use it as my table, lay it on the floor before me and the portable heater, me and the small black and white TV, and eat microwavable meals. I looked at the plank with new eyes: happy, determined, do-what-I-say eyes. I used a glue gun to stick all the bits of a paper plate to the board, and then, noticing that I still had five tubes of glue left, kept pressing the trigger and sealing over the bits until I was out. I was out of paint, too. I was out of India ink, out of crayons, and thinking that this would be it, the end of my plastic efforts, my last work, so nice, curt, pretty, and finally over. Going to the fridge to grab a bottle of Carta Blanca, I noticed a red vial of food coloring. Back when I was dating Meg, when she had taken an Elementary teaching job to patch up our no money situation, she had baked Valentine's Day cookies for her kids. The second graders ate them, but she made too many and had to bring a tin container of them back to the apartment. After a week, we threw them away, but there was some of that food coloring left over. I was never going to do anything else with it, so I poured the red liquid over the hot swirls of hardening glue and lifted the work, tilting and positioning the wood until the trapped food coloring had slowed and finally saturated the piece. And it *was* a piece. More, I knew it was art.

USUALLY, I BRING A book to Phoenix. Right now, I'm into all that crime pulp that Goddard was hip to and tried to make heady with slow pans and jump cuts, all that shadow junk I take for granted when I walk down the sketchy length of a tenebrous alley and feel like I'm being filmed without getting paid or lauded for my efforts. I was reading a too-smooth edition of *The Moon in the Gutter*, and it was going fast. This was one of those books I'd been rereading for years because reading it felt like the best, most insane points of watching TV. I was on page thirty-seven when I heard the door chime open.

This guy who looked like he could have been in high school or college—well, he looked like he was at a stage in his developing persona where he could pass for anything but respectable—walked in and moved toward the front desk. He was wearing all black, but I didn't think he was trying to look cool or fashionably nihilistic in his black T-shirt and faded black jeans. Even his goddamn hair was black. He was cute, wide-eyed, and had a future despite himself. He looked like he got by on his appearances but was unaware of that blessing. I tensed up because no one ever came into Phoenix this early, or if they did, they were housewives searching for bamboo frames that went with their futons or kids trying to waste time before walking home from school. "Are you guys accepting applications?"

"Oh, yeah. I guess we probably are." Relieved that he would be gone soon and I could go back to my David Goodis, I tore an application from a sheaf by the register and handed it to the guy. He said thanks, and I could smell all this tequila on his breath. There it is, I thought, that's the reason I stick to beer. This guy smelled like his body was holding onto its foreign poison for reasons of self-preservation. He sounded like he had a cold.

"Thanks, man." He looked as if he wanted to just hang out, be a part of the scene. The guy turned to the wall of high school art, bobbing and nodding his head like he was dealing with his hangover with tiny jerks and it was a method he was used to. I went back to the book and read the same paragraph over and over, not looking up at him, wishing he would leave.

At the Bolo Lounge, I saw Church's ex, Sharon. Again, I found her attractive, and again, I was mad at myself for being so weak. Sharon was alone. If I stuck around, I was going to have to talk to her. I just wanted to leave, but leaving would mean definite eye contact when I walked over to the bar to pay up. I hate thinking that some women are hot or hot and available. The guy behind the bar was smiling at her, and he had that "stick around, drinks will be cheap" magnet charm that looks disgusting from the tables. Well, from *my* table. I wasn't glaring their way, but I was looking, and the bartender noticed, stopped his zero-headed flirty gestures, and pointed so that Sharon could turn and look at me. Before she slid around on the barstool, I saw the bartender mouth a *"You know this guy?"* Sharon looked at me and smiled big, turned back to the bartender, and two minutes later, walked over to my table with two brown bottles of beer. I didn't really know Sharon. I'd just seen her and not spoken to her enough times to form silent opinions that shifted in accordance with what she was wearing or how drunk I let myself become. I looked down at the napkin that I'd been scribbling over, and she sat across from me.

"Hey," she said after scooting the open beer bottle over so that it was directly under my nose, "you work for my husband, Church."

I looked at her, looked at the bottle, lifted it to my lips for a sip, then said, "I thought the two of you were separated." She was a pretty woman, what the hell did I think I was fighting anyway?

"We are. I'm not holding out any hope that he'll want me to move back in with him, but he is my husband, and I'm going to call him that until someone stops me."

"Yes, err—"

"Sharon."

I acted as if I didn't know her name for no real reason. I guess I wanted to hear her say it aloud. "Sharon, thanks for the beer, but is there something I can help you with?"

"You work with Church, and I miss him. I understand, or I have conned myself into feeling okay with his decision to leave me for..."

"For himself."

"Yeah, for himself. But I worry about him and want to know what he's up to, what he looks like, how he's holding up. Church comes in here every three nights. When he does, we talk, but it's nothing, just compliments and well-wishes. I smile, but it hurts me how much he doesn't seem to have needed me at all." She took a sip of her beer, looked soft with old pain, then smiled a smile that was supposed to say *I'm fine, I feel like this at least twice a day, and I'm managing.* Sharon cleared her throat and said, "Church comes into Bolo whenever he wants, and it's a crapshoot as to whether or not we are even going to talk. But you, you're here every night right after work. I can meet you here. I can buy you a few drinks, and you can tell me about my husband."

I slept like a baby suckling on a pacifier steeped in absinthe. I slept as well as when Meg and I first got together. Her smile of grace and wanting, and me wishing I could thank her for being allowed to roll around with her on the blanketed floor, sleep, and wake with her and just praise the comfort. Here is Meg with warm, well-muscled thighs, short pixie legs that hung over me in the night, and in the dark, I could stare until my eyes adjusted to her mouth clicking and pouting dream-pouts. Or some nights, when it was really cold, there was a plug-in heater set before of us, and I'd look at her in the electric orange light. I slept like that because it was hard to keep justifying my worry over a job that paid nothing and sometimes got on my nerves. because letting Sharon buy me a few drinks after work might end up saving me thirty dollars a week. Because, when I relaxed and wasn't tense with unguarded misanthropy, I found Sharon a pleasure to look at, to think of.

WHEN I GIVE UP shaving and getting haircuts, I sign up for a world of silent derision. If there is no style I'm aiming for, when I let my hair start to go bushy and don't even bother to clean up the sideburns, I get stared at. My stubble comes in a little thicker on the right. My hair is all around black, not as black as the hair on that dude who asked me for an application, but black enough. My beard comes in with flecks of blonde and red. It looks like I'm too cheap to go to the barber or like some recent event has done exacting damage, burnt my self-respect and left me with uneven sideburns. I liked getting all hairy; it was always the first thing I did whenever I got a new job, and it could only help my situation with Church. We hadn't been too friendly for a while, just him saying "hi" when he entered Phoenix Framing and then me saying "later" as I left. As my hair grew out, I noticed that Church was getting more comfortable around me, we weren't talking any more than usual, but he seemed more at ease. Once I decided to do the job for Sharon, I knew I could play this up, act like I was moving toward his way of thinking and being. This just meant I would mess my hair up with my fingers before he walked into the store and keep stretching whenever he looked my direction. I was already wearing a lot of dirty white T-shirts and the same pair of blue jeans every day.

Church came in a little early. He was holding a small potted Aloe vera plant. I put down my paperback copy of *Roughneck*. Church nodded hello to me as he walked over to the counter and set down his plant. He smelled like hummus and spilled coffee. He asked how we'd done this morning. I said we had sold another goddamned Munch print to some teenager.

"Which print?"

"You know. The only one," I said then opened my mouth and bugged out my eyes for a few seconds to make fun of *The Scream.*

"That's funny, kid. Let's go outside."

He put the BACK IN TEN MINUTES sign up on the door then and, leaning against the dumpster behind the store, lit up a joint. I was drinking a bottle of mineral water, hoping he wouldn't ask me if I wanted to take a hit, but he was a good guy, and there was no way he wouldn't offer. Church lifted his stick in my direction and raised his left eyebrow. I said, "Thanks, man, but my throat is sore. I'm also going to the Bolo later. I don't want to be that messed up when I get there. I'm afraid of going sloppy and making an ass out of myself." It was all lies except for the part about the Bolo Lounge. If I had left that detail out, I would have sounded like I was hiding something.

"Well, Church, what's with the plant?"

He didn't say anything, so I pushed on a little. I mean, I *had* to have something to tell Sharon. This had nothing to do with any snitcher's work ethic, and I just couldn't take sitting in front of Sharon and having to tell her what I *thought* was going on with Church. Plus, I didn't want to make up any anecdotes.

"Aloe vera plants are as ugly as sea creatures in an H.P. Lovecraft short story."

"Yeah, but I owe them a lot."

"How do you mean?"

"I used to get paper cuts all the time. I've always drawn pictures—I don't know if you knew that about me—and for the last five years, my favorite surface has been plain white typing or copy machine paper. I used to like the look of straight black lines on this too-white paper, but I was bad at handling the sheets and would get these sharp paper cuts along my wrists and the flesh between thumb and forefinger. I hate antiseptics, so Sharon would have to slice up Aloe vera plants for me and, for a long time, I never thought of them as anything but a balm for my art. Now that Sharon and I aren't together and she's not around to take care of the plants or my cuts, I figure I should take them out of the ground and bring them into the shop. Give them to anyone who might want one."

"But what do you do when you get a paper cut?"

"I don't get paper cuts anymore. I don't use copy paper anymore. I use manila."

I met Sharon as I said I would, all the while knowing that I would have been at the Bolo Lounge anyway. Understanding my actions and my poisonous seat in the world of people, my habits and my intentions, calmed me in a way that booze never could. Drink just made me angry, and if I was addicted to anything, it was that rush of distaste and my acquiescence of that distaste. I liked feeling so mad that I couldn't move. I liked that blockhead hurt. Was it too late for me? *Sure it is*, I thought, *you're done, you're stiff, you give off the smell of sealed glue, of muscles that are no good to cook and eat.* There was no sadness in that knowledge. There was little comfort, but there was no sadness.

I ARRIVED AT BOLO at the same time I always got there: ten minutes after work, the space of time it took for me to walk over to the bar, circle the block looking for a discarded newspaper, maybe pick it up or maybe leave it on the ground, then go back to the bar. It was the same routine as all the other nights, but I felt like I was early. I ordered a drink, a real drink. "Scotch. Rocks." When the bartender asked me what kind of Scotch, I didn't even say, "Whatever you think is good," or, "Surprise me," but stayed quiet as he poured and asked for my three bucks. I gave him a five and walked over to my table. My table. Yeah, it was my table. Those were my palm prints all over the waxy wood; this was a cigarette that I picked off the floor and let rest on a cardboard coaster.

Sharon came in and sat down at my table. She was wearing her hair in a bun now, trying to look like the sexy old, the confident, the precise, and unmovable. I knew it was because, in her mind, she now owned Church. Maybe I hadn't sold him out directly, but that's only because there was no loyalty in me to begin with. Sharon's skin was an expensive cream, a hard to find porcelain. Her hazel eyes looked heavy with mascara, but they weren't; they just looked that way. Sharon was a beauty, and I felt like telling her.

"You know, I think Church is an idiot for not being with you. There's no way he can do any better."

Sharon smiled. I could see the lines at the corners of her mouth crimp and create the face she would have when she was Church's age. It didn't look bad. It looked powerful, earned.

"So you don't think my husband can do any better, huh? Not even with himself?"

"Not even with." I tried to repeat her words but felt dragged and spent. I smiled at Sharon and knew there was no way I could look as secure as she did. I felt over. "Do you know that you look like my…" I could have said favorite actress or cousin; whatever I said would have been a lie. Sharon looked like the girl I was currently attracted to, the girl I would think about till it hurt and humiliated me. I peered down at my drink and, still not even thinking about drinking, closed my eyes to breathe in the cheap Scotch fume. "Church is doing well. Church is…I'm glad he hired me." I slid the drink over to her, then got up and walked to my apartment.

Once indoors, I stood still for a minute, then lowered myself onto the floor, a tired animal. The room was dusk-dark, and I wasn't going to turn on any lamps. My eyes would adjust, and I would be fine. If I absolutely couldn't stand the grey-blue of my apartment, I'd light up a goddamned candle. I was exhaustd, but it wasn't even close to physical fatigue. It wasn't mental stress either, although flecks of what felt like hungry synapses were snapping and washing their alarm throughout my cells. This was the feeling of lit Roman candles being held like a wand over the skin. It almost felt good. I relaxed on my chest and spread my arms out over the cold floor, staring into the cracks between each tile. How could I ever say I was safe from art? Everywhere I looked, there was a crumb of black chalk, a bit of broken pencil lead.

WHEN I SHOWED UP for work the next day, the guy who took an application was waiting outside the store, ready to turn it in. I could see him from three blocks away, could see that he was wearing all black again. I slowed my pace, hoping that he'd leave, but he wasn't going anywhere.

"Hey," he said.

"Hey."

As I opened the shop and walked over to get around the register counter, the guy, after quietly entering the establishment, just stood all soldier-like by the door, ready for war, ready to pull his life together and get a job. It looked as if he had even shaved his face and brushed his hair.

"I just wanted to turn in this application, man."

"Sure. I'll give it to the boss."

"Great. What time does he come in, by the way?"

"He comes in later. Look, don't worry, man, I'll make sure he gets it."

"Cool."

Then again, as he did before, the applicant wanted to hang around the store, but this time, he stuck his face right up against the wall of art, studying the marker lines and daubs of tempera. I looked at him looking at the art. I hadn't brought a book with me. There was no tequila smell coming from his direction. "I really like this one," he said. "This one that is, I think, a leg or a trombone. Who did it?"

"I don't know."

The guy pulled the framed piece off the hook on the wall and tilted it against his chest to spy a signature. "Who is Church?"

Your new boss. "I don't know, but you've got to put that back on the wall."

"Sorry man." He *did* look sorry, didn't want to hurt his chances of getting hired. With over-gentle care, he placed the drawing back on its hinge, said his, "Thanks, appreciate it" and left. Three seconds after he closed the door, the drawing fell off the wall. I shut my eyes in blink-reflex when I heard the cracking sound, then kept them shut for three calm-down seconds. When I walked over to the sheet of manila, I saw that the actual work was fine. The problem was the frame, shattered glass and scraped metal, the most expensive part of the piece, the borders that turned hasty charcoal lines into something for which Church could charge money. I pulled the drawing out from under the shards, rolled it into a tube, and put a rubber band around it.

I swept up the broken glass into a dustpan but stopped before dumping the bits into the wastebasket. After a few moments of proper hesitation, I poured the broken glass back out onto the floor, right into the empty black frame. Then I stepped onto the pile of glass until there were no more crunching sounds, swayed my foot forward to send the bits sliding across the linoleum, and walked over to the counter to write out a note for Church: *Hey, Boss, I had to take off early. I tried to call you, but no one answered. Some dude put in an application. Seems like a cool guy.*

I went over to the register and took out a twenty dollar bill, stuffed it into my front blue jean pocket, lifted the rolled up drawing, and left.

TWO DAYS HAVE PASSED, and there won't be a reason to leave the apartment for at least another three. Years of living alone, interrupted only by the occasional live-in romance, have taught me the value of non-perishables food items. I've got cans of lentil soup, tins of sardines, packages of cereal in the cupboard, plus all these crackers. Since I haven't had the desire to go out and get a drink, I haven't had the desire to go out at all. I'm on the floor, my legs crossed, but not in a lotus or kindergarten-style; my feet dangle or my feet point—they go numb from the cramped way I'm seated. I arch them, wiggle toes, and the feeling comes back.

There is a message on the answering machine. I was sitting just so and drinking a can of Dr. Pepper last night when I let the tape take it, staring at the drawing I swiped and have now tacked to the wall. "Hey, I need to talk to you. Call or come by the store...I'm not mad at you...come by, okay." I think: *It's cool that you're not mad, Church. I'd go by and pick up my last paycheck, but I just can't tell you when I will be walking into a store, not just yours, any store at all, not for a while because I have lots to keep me busy.*

I have nubs of charcoal that are as small as an infant's pinkie nail and number two pencils gleaned from between the tiles. I have black markers divined from kitchen drawers, the thick suckers that stink up the room with headache-inducing odors and seem never to go dry. I have a bar of deodorant that leaves wonderful smears on cardboard and twenty dollars' worth of Manila paper that I picked up as I walked away from my duties at Phoenix. These are not art supplies. This is not art. I'm drawing what Church was drawing. Church wasn't drawing a leg or a set of hips. On all those yellow legal pads, and on those dozen Post-It notes, Church was drawing *drawing*. Church was describing an act. Having achieved a level of confidence, Church even decided to frame that description. The lines and trip marks look like what they have no choice but to look like. These that I am doing now *could* perhaps be arms, but they could be *anything,* and that would depend on whoever was looking.

My boss has been calling today, but every time he gets the machine, he hangs up. This is probably stressing him out. He feels guilty because he has already hired my replacement. Late morning and the kid in black is probably cutting up boxes in the alley behind the store. Tomorrow, if Church calls again, I will answer the phone and let him officially can me. I'll thank him for hiring me in the first place, thank him for putting up with me, say absolutely nothing about the bigger mercy because Church is no teacher; he couldn't even point out a way.

Church is happy being alone, happy giving up his wife and his Aloe vera plants. Hey, I am *not* happy giving up anything. There isn't a string of moments that pass by without grief, thoughts about how I've done foul things, unleashed the rankest vibes, ruined good fortune, and spoiled my chances at grown-up peace. I've had three serious relationships, and after things blew up, I never kept in touch. I have let down every friend and employer with thoughtless moves and panicky drink and the general passivity that ensues. People don't forgive, or if they do, it's because there is something they get out of pardoning. I ride toward that basic revelation with every mark that I make and wonder how I will sustain this ride. What vehicle rocks along and accepts these mistakes, these attempts at erasure as a state, a kind?

Meg, my last ex, is probably dating someone seriously, maybe not drawing pictures with the guy, but probably planning a future. Alternatively, she is already married, or she just doesn't care anymore. Sharon has to be at the Bolo Lounge. Church is most likely there, too, and now they're both talking about me.

"God, I can't believe you hired that guy. Who knows what else he might have taken from you?"

"Yes, he let me down, but nobody's all bad. If I was the kind of man who believed in prayer...."

I set a tiny piece of charcoal on a plain sheet of clean manila. There is nothing glib in me. No jokes or desire as I press the sheet down with my left palm, put my right thumb over the bit of black chalk, hold my breath and exhale as I push my thumb down the surface and spend the black over the humble grain. The line is too straight; it looks silly and stubborn, but it looks like itself. I blow the dark dust from the sheet and, still staring at the fact of the line, feel around for another bit of chalk.

The Fight for Space

I am starting to hate Batman, all that revenge in the blood and the vigilantism he gets away with, the luxury of his guilt and the costume that expresses his staid vendetta. Batman gets laid, too: Catwoman, Batgirl, and the daughters of his enemies. Plus, no matter what, Batman is at core a schizophrenic do-gooder, potentially as dangerous as the forces he aims to thwart. No matter what, Batman is still Bruce Wayne, billionaire philanthropist, sack of shit crybaby, with the mansion and the butler doting after him.

There is a girl at my work who doesn't take care of her kids. I mean she takes basic food-and-shelter care of them, and they go to church and carnivals and get Happy Meals, but they don't call her mommy; they call her June, and June likes to say that she's more of a big sister than a mommy. June has two pretty little girls, both of them always drawing pictures of cars and balloons, smiling and trying to impress everyone in the office, aged seven and five, and June is twenty-three. June's mom knew the boss, cashed in a shadowy favor, and got him to hire her teenage daughter when the young woman needed to have work and immediate structure, right after she got pregnant (the first time) and quit high school. June gets paid well, too, like manager money, and I guess she does her work and customers like her. She even came out in the commercial we did for the Spanish channel. Everybody who sees it thinks June is a blonde-haired woman because she bleaches her hair, and the commercial was shot in a frosted light. June comes to work early and talks to the car insurance sales girl next door, and when her kids are sick or not in school, she brings them in for the day. June's kids smile and never say anything; everyone thinks they're beautiful, and they are.

Batman's trophy room pisses me off the most; it's like our hero does not want to find peace. There is a dinosaur in that room and costumes of every psycho-nut-job he ever caught. There is an oversized Joker card, a gigantic penny, and a glass display of all the Robin outfits. How do you meditate or get clear in a cave like that, with a wall-sized computer screen and bloody capes hanging off swivel chairs?

June's husband manages a Chinese restaurant. I've never seen him, but I've heard her talk with the guy. She was smoking a cigarette and leaning against the white pickup he lets her drive, holding a cell phone to her ear as I pulled a dolly steeped with clock radios and toasters into the back of the store: "You don't support me, Vic." The rest of the day, June was silent. Most of the time, June kids around that she shouldn't have gotten married, her man is a loser, wants to do nothing but hang out with his uncles and tell jokes, listen to cumbias, and go to cantinas. Vic isn't a drinker, and he is never drunk, but the kind of fun he has when he is out with Jaime and Frank is something June can never offer him.

Every time, no matter where you see any legitimate Batman merchandise, you see the words created by Bob Kane somewhere on it. Bob Kane was kind of the creator, for sure the man who got paid, but there is another man named Bill Finger, a shoe salesman Bob Kane knew from high school. When the superhero character Kane was trying to pitch wasn't going so well, Bill Finger stepped in and came up with the ideas that informed the first salable sketch work for The Dark Knight, the notion that The Batman should look more like an actual bat, don a cape, have slits for eyes, and be a darker creature altogether. Bob Kane's original Batman looked kind of like Zorro with a Da Vinci flying machine strapped to his shoulders. Bill Finger wrote the first published Batman story and came up with most of Catwoman, Two-Face, The Riddler, the look of the Joker, and the Batcave itself. Bill Finger never got any real credit and was always kissing up to Bob Kane, even as he sharpened his boss's rough work and offered the comic book world some of its creepier, more endearing plot twists. At the end, Bill Finger could no longer be trusted to turn in assignments on time and died an alcoholic wreck. Ask anyone with a casual interest in The World's Greatest Detective, and chances are, the fan won't know Bill Finger. I only know of him because of a tiny article in a comic book fanzine.

Sometimes I would look at June and wonder why she wasn't sleeping around. June was just a kid when she got knocked up and married. June is attractive, and I think she must be dressed in whatever the style of the season is because I am surprised by the varieties of her outfits, although I admit to knowing nothing about what goes on at shopping malls or inside catalogs. I have never seen her flirt with anyone ever, and June is a pretty woman. Her brown skin and regal nose and the smile that is always a surprise to me, how warm I can feel when I see it erupt before me.

When I was fifteen, I hung out with a twenty-five-year-old college dropout named Scott. Scott was a friend to anyone who didn't run off when he wanted to "just talk, kill time, whatever." Scott did his hair all bleach-black, wore Misfits and Skinny Puppy T-shirts, and shared a jumpy vernacular with the high school kids who kept his company. Scott was a recovering alcoholic pill-popper who would jack off all the time to maintain sobriety, and sometimes Scott would relapse and be so hung over that he would ask me if I could help him sell comic books at a table he rented in the City Wide Garage Sale. Comic books were totemic props Scott used to kick his low times. Lots of nights, I'd be walking back from his home and think of Scott with his plans for the evening: "Man, I've got all these Dr. Doom and Sand Man." I didn't know anything about the characters, good, bad, or Wolverine. It would have been such a project to understand any one of them, so many self-referential issues, all of them stringing you along to get back issues or subscribe. I didn't like that Scott sold these comics to kids who had to pull at their parents for money. Scott would charge at least a buck more than whatever the cover price was, even if he stole them, even if they were genuinely worthless, not even of kitsch value. The comic books almost *never* moved, and it was like Scott was wasting his day, but then some kid with five bucks and a mom looking at secondhand silverware would stop at Scott's stand, and ten minutes later, Scott would send me out to buy two cheeseburgers at the Whatever Burger across the street.

There are several dirt alleys that crisscross behind my house, and it's safe and wonderful at night to walk the soft earth path and see the lights from the houses. This neighborhood in which I live is drowsy with comfort: elderly ladies who want to show me pictures of their granddaughters and kids walking around all worry-brow, door to door, looking for dogs they always find because the dogs want to come back. I walk the alleys to get to my favorite bar because the march sets up my mood, becomes this sneaky operation wherein a 9 p.m. stroll can turn into a 3 a.m. cab ride. My lips fight a grin all the way to The Freeze Lounge, and when I get there, the grin just happens, spreads on my face and stays, and I feel as if I've got secrets for sale.

Last week, I encountered the man I am calling Pinser Selby. I could feel that some presence was walking behind me, not too fast, as if whoever was tailing me was going to suddenly appear up close, and we'd meet that nervous point where one of us would have to say hello or just be a jerk. I stopped walking and leaned against a wooden fence, pretending that I was standing by my place. I waited for him to pass me and thought I was pulling off the ruse. I mean, *I* was buying the scene, even thought I could call out for an imaginary wife, just make up a name and say, "Hey, Penny, could you come out and help me with the trash?" or, "Yo, Selma, you left the goddamned hose on again!" I would have said *something,* but when the guy was close enough to hear me, to casually receive my misinformation, I saw his shadow. The head looked wrong, elongated, then sharp and curved on the ground, appeared to me, for a quick nothing, like the profile of a cartoon duck. So I looked up and saw that the walker was wearing some kind of WWII gas mask with those saucer-black spheres for eyes and that salt shaker nose.

I think I opened my mouth, and I know I didn't shut my eyes because there was my face all twisted into the saucers' reflection, the color of my skin and the color of all the night behind me, but no features. Pinser Selby turned his headgear back to the alley and kept walking.

In return for helping out whenever I could, Scott paid me in comic books, which I really didn't want or need and always made the worst choices about accepting. I wasn't into any of the hero stories, and who the hell were the villains? One Sunday afternoon, while Scott was sleeping in his parents' Volvo, I was left in charge of his table and ended up making him fifty bucks by being nice and not creeping anyone out with total knowledge of all the issues and themes. Someone would ask me a question about Dr. Fate or Ant Man, and I would say, "Beats me, but everything is on sale for the next thirty minutes." Scott was so grateful, even though all I had done was stand and wait for the money to change. "Here, man, grab any book you want, maybe get one that will go up in value, first of a series, limited release." I chose a comic book that was wrapped in special edition plastic and intended to be the reintroduction of a venerable but barely popular character to a generation of potential fans. Scott suggested that I leave the comic book in its sleeve, never read it, and then try to sell it in ten years. I knew there was no way I'd be able to manage an operation like that. When I thought of how I might never read the comic book and how if I didn't rip the seal open right away, I would die without ever knowing who this character was, I started to panic.

The Pinser was a Silver Age "Metal Man from Lurnao 6." He had the same bodybuilder look like all the other superheroes of his time, with a cape flowing from his neck and something over the head to obscure his face, in the Pinser's case, a helmet that aided in his space and time travel. On his home planet, the Pinser was an environmentalist whose main preoccupation was locating and preserving the Kasul trees before the entire Kasul Forest was laid to lumber. There were constant little, pointless wars happening on Lurnao 6, and there were beings that did whatever the hell they wanted with the land. That was okay with the pirate world of Lurnao 6; in fact, Lurnaos 1-5 depended on the trees, furs, oil, and general largesse of the Pinser's home world. They tended to encouraging the political confusion of Lurnao 6. Such ubiquitous strife could only keep the price of Kasul trees and their coveted sap down.

For the Pinser, it was all about the trees. He would do anything to preserve them. Most of the time, the Pinser was with the good guys, the sentinels that chased down Nazi brains over a cartoon Europe and foiled kidnappers before time could take its nick. When the good guys didn't seem too good to him, the Pinser went with any group that would cater to his cause. Often, the Pinser was portrayed as a selfish, solipsistic, eccentricity of a hero, and many times he was supposed to be totally evil, getting in the way of the legitimate two-dimensional players, slowing down their action for these goddamned trees. Other than that, the Pinser was not around.

It took me forever to get out of university. I kept taking "breaks" and never understood that accepting guaranteed loans was about eventually securing a job. I ended up with a double major and like three minors. Nothing, I mean *nada-zero,* I could use in my future unless I wanted to stay within the hermetic hamster-wheels of my subjects and try to teach somewhere. I chose to write my undergraduate honors thesis on "non-authoritative" superheroes, how they fared in their pulp worlds, when and at what point their sales might peak, and what it meant that you could always, no matter how lame the prequels and sequels, just do another ManMan cartoon, ManMan movie, ManMan rock song, ManMan TV show. I did as much research as I wanted; all my sources were primary. In my quasi-legitimate furor, I spent half of my Pell Grant on comic books and Wizard magazines. I chose to write the dissertation in an aphoristic style because I wanted my ingots of epiphany to bounce off each other, resound, and ricochet with Nietzschean spite and sing-song, and because I couldn't figure out how to do footnotes on my laptop. I read ten pages of what I had titled "Culled for the Cape: Towards The Shamed Shaman" at an end-of-the-semester honors party. Everyone assumed I got the title and trajectory from my thesis advisor, a man known for his liberal use of alliteration and an earth science reading of soap operas. However, it was all my work, and I was proud. I showed slides and was a big hit with the twelve people in attendance.

I wasn't looking at anyone in the appliance store anymore. I couldn't talk to the customers in the front, but I was cool with the supervisors in the back because everything we ever said was about the supplies we had ordered, what was coming in, and what needed to be pushed to another place—"Can you move this over here? Can you make space for these?"

It was a situation where I dreamt, woke, worked, and dreamt. The more I tossed myself into silent duty, the more it looked like I was a good worker and the more I was encouraged to take as many breaks as I needed. I was forever hanging out at the convenience store next door. One Wednesday morning as I tried to decide what color of Powerade to purchase, I saw my old boss/buddy Scott in town again. I hadn't seen him in ten years, and here he was, different now. Scott didn't really look like he had aged much, but he was fatter, love handles and belly tucked into his khakis and starched shirts. Scott was at the pay counter, scratching off the three-dollar lotto, smiling. I heard him mumble an, "Oh, well," before walking out of the store. What did he do for a living now? Scott looked like a high school teacher. I checked out his car as he pulled out and drove away. There was a GO HAWKS sticker on the bumper and a plastic parking clip hanging from the rearview mirror. Damn. It was not easy for me to assume that this guy who, in his mid-to-late twenties, used to sleep with fifteen-year-old Goth chicks might now be teaching composition to freshmen. I didn't think he would allow himself to be qualified for any other type of work.

June was taking suspiciously long lunch breaks, showing up to work looking like she was going to a bar. Everything about her was tweaked toward the sexy, the cautious, never ready to give any information about what was happening in her life, how her girls were doing, always a quick, "Good, fine," whenever anyone asked. I never asked.

If I were eating at Popeyes or McDonald's, I would have to fight an impulse to pull the Sharpie out from my clipboard and write BILL FINGER on the table wherever I sat. I kept believeing that if I just wrote the man's name, a statement would ensue, like BILL FINGER WROTE BATMAN or NO BILL FINGER, NO BATMAN. There is only an ephemeral truth in any declarative strictness, especially when centered over this shy and drunken cat that would bow, *literally bow* whenever Bob Kane entered a room. I could never write down his name. I could come real close: I would hold the permanent marker over the cleanest place on a table and whisper, *"Bill Finger,"* then force a cough and get up to throw my lunch trash away and get the hell out of wherever I was trying to eat.

Scott was in my life again, and when I looked at him, I just felt like he owed me money or time or slices of an education never garnered. I'd see him at the Stop-n-Go next door to our office almost everyday. He would drive up in his silver Honda and get out and buy cigarettes and a pack of Lifestyles. I would be behind him in line or looking at the breakfast tacos under the heat lamp, and Scott would be pressing himself a fountain drink or flipping the pages of a *Maxim* or *Men's Health*. I don't think he recognized me; I mean, he never looked my way, or if he did, he tried to cover up any click of recognition. After Scott paid for his items, he would sit in his car and wait for a parked pickup to slowly move behind him. I knew that pickup, and there was never a moment when I doubted that a fork-in-the-road influence on my life was messing around with a married woman.

The collector's issue I was compelled to rip open and read was my introduction to the Pinser. The comic book was called *The Fight for Space*, and it was totally wordless, no text, all these fuchsia and mud renderings of our hero in stillness and sudden flight, his sense of slow panic and sudden serenity. "The Metal Man from Lurnao 6" was reintroduced to A.D. Comics with no showiness and a complete humility towards the Silver Age Icon. Well, "icon" is maybe too *sure* a word, the Pinser was never a fanboy favorite, but he was this very real specter that haunted the borders of the entire A.D. universe. There were twelve pages that taught me to understand this brooding monk of a creature. With his legs crossed, his head lolling, surrounded by alien flora, rubbing his gloved hands together, and—in the last panel of the comic—sensing enough danger to raise his head, to look for those who might oppose him, to observe and admit to a readiness for action.

Shaken by the man in the gas mask, I needed to get to my bar more than ever, but it looked like that's where the man in the gas mask was headed. I walked behind him, always thirty feet away, and when the alley road met The Freeze Lounge parking lot, I stopped and hid behind the shadows of a cypress tree. The man pulled off his headgear, rubbed the back of his neck, and then walked into the bar. I counted for twenty-eight seconds, then went inside. The Freeze Lounge was dead and dark, save the little red candles at every table, and probably three people, and one of whom was the guy who entered with a gas mask under his arm.

I sat at a table where I could stare at him but, if caught, turn my head to the dartboards where women usually stood. Here, I studied the man. He was, I thought, in his fifties, a strong looking fellow, small but tough, tight shoulders bound by his yellow sports coat. His hair was completely white and, considering that he had just been wearing a gas mask, surprisingly kempt. The man was talking to the bartender; they got along and looked like they knew each other well. The guy kept calling the bartender Jules, and after he paid up for his three Cosmopolitans and yanked his gas mask from the floor by his bar stool, the bartender said, "See you, Selby."

June and Scott were a definite item. For a week, I was the only one who knew anything about the affair, but then everyone knew, and there was no hiding the fact. June moved herself and her kids into her mom's house and then asked the boss for a payday advance so she could get her own apartment: "The kids will stay with my mom. I need a place to think." It was an ugly, unstable scene for a week, with June's mom dropping by and everyone clearing out to let them talk to each other, phone calls that the receptionists were instructed not to answer. June would scream into her cell and then leave work early; she would show up to work late, and nobody could tell her anything. Then, whatever the separation was, it found a rhythm of resignation. Vic sent flowers to the office two times, but when he realized he wasn't going to get his wife back, he made sure he got his truck. Scott started coming by to pick her up from work. Everyone was cool with him, thought he was a nice guy with a smart job and that he and June looked good together, respectable.

I followed Pinser Selby as soon as he walked out The Freeze Lounge. I followed him as if I was in love with him. I followed him as if I wanted to kill him. Careful all the way, I walked behind the man for half a mile of alleys and sidewalks before I saw him cross a street to get to a convenience store. A car was pulling in to get some gas, slowed down before the pump, then whoever was inside saw the man in the gas mask and decided to fill up somewhere else. Pinser Selby pulled the gear off his head and entered the gas station. He was smiling at the clerk. He was a handsome old guy with pals everywhere it seemed, and he talked to the clerk for five minutes before walking outside with a pack of cigarettes. He placed his headgear by his feet and, standing outside the store, smoked two cigarettes before bending down to pick up his gas mask.

In my house, there is heat when I want heat and cold when I want cold. There are candles, an unplugged box fan, and a six-pack of Diet Pepsi in the fridge that I accidentally bought and will never drink. There is running water, and there are books that I have not read but *plan* to read. There are pennies in a plastic Jack o' Lantern, and when Halloween comes around, I'll let the kids grab a fistful each. I've got towels in the bathroom, TV dinners in the freezer, and Felix the Cat cartoons on videocassette. I do my bills, and I do push-ups. I try to fit into the same clothes year after year, and I even have two posters of my favorite actresses, Natalie Wood and Ingrid Bergman. In my house, there is *pattern* if not reason, a life that very nearly sustains its own breathing. Outside my house, there is a man who walks the blocks and wears a gas mask, a man who talks to bartenders and convenience store clerks with an ease I have never cultivated, let alone come close to mastering. Pinser Selby scared the shit out of me when I saw him in the alley, and whoever drove off without filling up must have felt a similar frisson. I ached with curiosity; I couldn't rest until I tracked the man down, surmised his route, and did the gumshoe work. The dude in the car drove away. Anyone else might freak and call the cops, even though there might be no way to articulate a complaint to the proper authorities. The more radical elements of any neighborhood watch program might feel the compulsion to crust into a cabal. Who could blame them?

When I was the only one who knew about June and Scott, I held a quiet power but did not enjoy the rush of their secret show or the pangs of my special insight. I was in a dangerous place *for them.* I mean, I could have threatened, postponed, even moved their worlds toward other poles. I could have come up to June and told her whatever I knew of Scott, shown her pictures of how he used to dress, the swastika, bloody cross, "I'm a bad boy" T-shirts, tell her about the way he screwed me out of cash and bailed out of at least two engagements that I knew of. *Real scumbag, huh, June?* I could have run up to Scott while he was in line to buy condoms and said: *Hey, man, remember me? How long has it been? You live in town now? You're not going after that chick are you? I work with her and she is so married, kids and house, and a sister-in-law always stopping by the office, dropping off sushi in Styrofoam plates.* There was no way I would've said a word. Being witness to the smoldering seconds before a flame might take hold, I understood that it was not my place to snuff out any ember.

In the A.D. universe, the comic book citizens that are trying to get by, the comic book families and comic book nuns and comic book cheerleaders and comic book ex-cons that are just trying to live resent the superheroes that make it their absolute business to see that a comic book neighborhood or comic book city or comic book street junky is set right. Most of the A.D. superheroes are not welcomed and are met with at least an initial foreboding. The A.D. citizens seem to always shoot for a world without necessary defense, a place to be bored and measure everyday illumination, to weigh all quotidian joy, a place that characters like the Pinser were damned to worry over. In the A.D. universe, no hero is easily embraced. In the universe right outside my house, people fight for that exact space, that *distance*, all the time, everyday, and even go so far as to claim that the desire for such space and distance is not only a right, but an indelible part of being human. I have come to buy into and even participate in the bigotry of this belief, with my steady job and my lunch breaks away from the store and my decision to own a home. I find myself a champion of this very worldview. Still, *still*, I know I will never feel human unless I know that wherever Pinser Selby walks, he is safe. Batman always had help, even though his real hatred and the executions of his anger were totally his. There was Robin, Alfred, Commissioner Gordon, and Commissioner Gordon's beautiful redheaded daughter, and when it comes down to it, all of Batman's enemies were tripped up by their own quirks, their vanity or dour delusions; many times, the crazies caught themselves. Batman always had help. I have read every comic (and there are only fifty-two) in which "The Metal Man from Lurnao 6" makes an appearance. Sometimes the Pinser saves the day; often he does not. But he never gets any help.

The Love You Belt

This was not my home with its outdated fixtures, risky electrical outlets, and creaks accompanying any step to the bathroom or broom closet. The quirks of negligible antiquity aside, I had signed the six-month lease for this place and was eager to deal with any secret squalor. Only, the rooms were totally clean; the kitchen counters shone with someone's elbow grease. The last occupant must have scrubbed down the walls, grated over the tiles with a toothbrush or a rough little rag, so there was nothing for me to do but nurse the shoulder pain of cleaning out the apartment from which I had just moved with cheap beer and fuzzy television. I tried to figure out what a cartoon bobcat was laughing at and sipped the mildest succor, knowing that I had been mentally set to spend the next two days sweeping, vacuuming, and spilling antibacterial liquid everywhere. Now all I could hope to do was pepper the floor space with the confetti of the commencing days.

Before I came to the house, I had thrown everything away, sold or donated my books and music, the clothes I no longer wore, the furniture that was always someone else's idea to purchase and push against a wall. I had spent four weekends cleaning out my receipts and outdated checkbooks. Now, wanting to scope out the neighborhood, I walked over to the Pronto Convenience Store down the block to take note of what kind of everything was sold. I almost bought a laminated map of the city, and I almost bought a yellow flashlight, but in the end, I purchased an eight-dollar six-pack of Corona, then went back to stretch my legs and take a shower.

This house was a space to start anew, get clean and prepare for an open future, decide how I felt about government and marriage, mark what target of belief and commitment over which I would drop my neglected degree. There was a world to attend to, but it was all in the head, idea-errands to execute or just kill. I came to this house with a duffel bag of blue jeans and black T-shirts, a plastic grocery sack of motel shampoos and Tic-Tacs, a fifteen-inch television, and the lust to be centered.

I did fifty-five sit-ups in front of a Betty Boop cartoon, courted the pleasure of feeling totally zapped, drank my beers, and then went to sleep.

THE NEXT DAY, MY postcards started to arrive, five in the box and nothing else, every one of them addressed to me, to this house, in my handwriting. Since I was old enough to think that looking at pictures on a wall was an adult project to cultivate, since I was into Veronica Lake movies, Felix the Cat cartoons, and photographs of Earth taken from outer space, I had collected postcards to quell the imp of a visual thirst. Postcards were my special hang-up, and I now made it my business to keep them. The few times I ever sent one out to just say HI or MISS YOU, I always ended up having to pay off the beads of embarrassment, intuitively understanding that HOPE YOU ARE OKAY or BE WITH YOU SOON declaratives marked in a curt or clumsy script never looked anything but desperate, or worse, a lie. Even if I *did* hope that some friend of mine was okay, even if I missed a girl to death and wanted to express my sucker longing to be with her as NOW as possible, the gesture seemed false. Plus, I got all torn up over the choice of postcard. Who would receive the promotional stills for *Spider Baby*? Who got Betty Page? It was stress, but not the kind that would stretch me wicked or even pull me toward punishing dreams.

I once dated a girl who never threw them away. Kelly saved all three TOGETHER FOREVER cards, just kept them after years of puppy love had gone shaggy-dog lousy. Even after we called it quits, Kelly still talked on the phone about how she saved the cards in a dresser drawer, along with her high school diploma and instant camera shots of her first trip to Spain. Then there was Samantha, "just a friend" for as long as that kind of ruse lasts, who had broken up with her long-term steady and came over to unwind and mouth unsubstantiated badness about the dude and try to get happy, get lost in the spun grandeur of our faux-fervent affections. Sam brought over a plastic grocery sack of candles, some flea market rune stones that looked like Jujubes, and an ear-shaped oyster shell she used as an ashtray. We talked like excited fourteen-year olds, listened to The Sisters of Mercy and Red Lorry Yellow Lorry, drank sales rack grocery store wine, pressed faces, and touched parts in the heady dark.

The next day, I felt bad; well, I felt shame, for myself, for Sam, and for the man with whom she would, no doubt, reunite, so I put into action the decision to ignore her. This behavior actually seemed adult to me. Samantha started to send me these FUCK YOU, BUM, I'VE BEEN CALLING ALL WEEK cards, then a host of I WANT TO SEE YOU AGAIN, *PLEASE*. DON'T IGNORE ME cards, then BE A MAN IF NOT A FRIEND cards. Slowly, as Samantha accepted the fate that we would not be friends at all or even speak again, the postcards stopped. Like a sap, I kept them, felt like I had to, like I owed it to her. Well, maybe not to her but to some anemic lacunae that might profit by my weakness before her. These cards were something to carry with me, a hair shirt to suffer beneath my everyday attire, a list of insults by which to be marked and measured, with which to rate humiliation. I stashed them away and avoided the cards just as I avoided her. As I prepared for the move, I found them in a shoebox of receipts and, without thinking, almost like a prolonged jerk-spasm reaction that my body had just now allowed itself to commit, I tossed them. I don't know if I felt free or capable of inward hurrahs, but with those babies gone, I was left with thirty-seven unmarked postcards, the ones I had purchased for myself, nothing written on them, never mailed, never even *ready* to be mailed. I put a stamp on each card and addressed them to my new residence, told myself that would be it, all the decoration allotted. My new place would be a Spartan ode to letting go, wherein the only hint of the life I'd once led, with its broken engagements, lost friends, and false career starts, would be these suspended postcards, kept for no reason, packed and preserved with every move, from bedroom to dorm room, efficiency to efficiency, and finally mailed to a blue-grey house and stuck on an off-white wall.

I MET MY NEIGHBOR Jonah a day after the first five postcards arrived. My car lights were on, and he jogged across the street to inform me of my carelessness. Jonah was a slight man with nothing in the way of a build but looked pent with doggie readiness and had an action-in-repossession aura about him. I mean, when I opened the door and saw him, I thought right away, *Where is the trouble, and what can I do to help?* With his milk-tin eyes and spiky tufts of uncombed hair, I could definitely believe whatever he said; my neighbor looked allergic to lies, if not a witness to absolute truth. I ran over to my Honda, "Man, thanks for the warning, Jack."

"It's Jonah, and I'd expect you to do the same for me." Later that night, heading over to the Pronto convenience store, I remembered that I had seen him before. Jonah was buying newspapers, a stack of Sundays at a buck fifty a pop. When I saw him hauling that pile of papers under his arms, I thought maybe this guy was affiliated with the news outfit, that maybe he had a column printed and wanted to clip it out, or there was a coupon he wanted lots of. Anyway, I figured the cat was crazy, bought my Pabst, and walked home. Now at the Pronto again, I was suddenly afraid to see him, even felt like I should speed my way out of the store. I got my six-pack, a plastic bag of peanuts, plus some coffee filters and started to walk back, moving quicker than I normally would, head down; if I walked into a parked car, then I would just deal with the accident and temper any ensuing pain. Whatever the effort, the two of us were neighbors and always in each other's view. We would eventually be friends or else be the kind of jumpy folk that avoid eye contact and maneuver to walk past one another without a word. Why should I have minded getting to know him? Yes, I came to this house to leave everything I was and could be nailed for; I had cut off from all my pals and only kept in touch with my immediate family. Didn't I have the right to make new friends and garner relations, however fleeting, however surrogate? Well, if not, then didn't I have the right to accept the fact of neighbors?

THE NEXT DAY, THERE were three more cards in my mailbox: a Raggedy Ann and two beach scenes. The doll looked haunted, and both shores seemed to picture the same limping palm tree, though they were different beaches shot at different times of the day. My postcards were slowing down. All counted, I had received twenty of them and was not yet at, but definitely approaching, the fear that the rest of my postcards had been lost in the mail. If that were the situation, I would welcome the inevitable atmosphere of mystery and loss, even cater to its vacuum. I knew that wasn't going to happen. I trusted the postal service, and I trusted that I would make rent on time and keep my lawn neat, my fence painted and waterproofed, and I trusted that if I made a friend, I would be okay. It was part of the move. The resolution to start again was never met with so much resolve and surrender. People could give me hell, and I wouldn't feel the burn, but that would never happen. I mean, where were the people?

Jonah was cooking barbecue. The block smelled of charcoal, lighter fluid, cooking meat, and insect repellant. I walked down to get my mail and saw him cooking by himself. Jonah looked totally domestic and family-oriented, but the thought of this man having a wife and kids just didn't seem right. I figured he was divorced or something; I mean, he seemed to be in his late-forties, and he had all those rooms, plus a storage shed sticking out from behind the house, and even a basketball hoop mounted over the garage door. I just assumed that Jonah once had a wife and she left him, taking whatever fools he might have fathered, and now Jonah was a broken man, buying too many Sunday papers, sitting on his porch and waiting for a neighbor to forget to turn off their car lights. Three more postcards left in the box: a gorilla, a dolphin, and a David Bowie. I smiled big and heard a, "Hey, neighbor, what the hell are you so happy about?" I turned to look at Jonah in a cooking apron, standing behind a smoky grill, waving his burger flipper at me. I was still smiling when he said, "Why don't you stop holding your dick and help me eat this food? My boss isn't going to show, and my brother-in-law was not invited."

"Yes, cool, let me put away my mail."

I ate a burnt hotdog and half an undercooked burger right by the grill, standing next to Jonah as he tried to even out the char on each patty and frank. We didn't say anything. Jonah offered me a Coke or a beer, and I said I'd drink a beer with him when he was done with all the meat. "Oh, hell," he said, then lifted a broken black and pink piece of ground chuck out of the pit and dumped it into a red dog bowl that said MAW. "As soon as he gets up from his nap," Jonah said, then kicked the bowl so the cooling meat settled and walked inside. I followed.

The air conditioner was on full blast even though the day was nice enough to have left the windows open. There was a smell of carpet cleaner and wet coffee grounds in a wastebasket; aromatherapy sticks gave off their plug-in stink meant to placate, to soothe. Jonah had a small portable TV with the sound turned down sitting on a TV tray, and on screen was a golf game. We got to his kitchen, and he yanked two beers out of the fridge, twisted the caps off, and put one in my face.

"Thanks."

"No sweat."

We sat down to the kitchen table as if we were going to get down to business, start playing cards, or pray over a meal. "What the hell is your name, man? I told you mine."

"Oh. It's Ouija. Like the ghost game, that board with the unnerving alphabet and the YES/NO."

"How did you score that tag?"

"My real name is Omar." Jonah waited for an elaboration, so I explained, "When I was a real little boy, too young to talk, I used to point at all kinds of stuff. Like, if there were adults talking, I would walk up to one of them and point at an object on their person, say a tie, a belt buckle, or a purse. Then I would look said victim in the eyes as if this was a heavy message, some serious information. I guess it was funny and somewhat creepy to people. A cousin of mine who was into Tarot cards and crystal necklaces would babysit me for teenager money and started calling me Ouija. It sounds like a kid name in a way."

Jonah looked like he was in the middle of a smile that never started. "My daddy was a preacher, and I guess he never wanted me to forget what this world could do to you if you let it." With that, Jonah got up from the chair. "You up for another, Ouija?"

"Sure thing, but after this one, I've got to fix up my place," which just meant that I was in the mood to tack up my postcards. I decided to pin them in my bedroom, on a wall where I might have otherwise placed a writing desk or a full-length mirror, across from where I might arrange my bed or stack any library books I might, over the course of the coming year, accrue. My postcards would be an inspiration. I could look at them while I lifted dumbbells or listened to NPR. I could look at them and find new worth in their populist design. Whenever I felt like moving them into a new pattern or arrangement, I wouldn't think twice. Do a cross, do a shoehorn pattern. King Kong and Dr. Doom: two-dimensional and triumphant. Conrad Veidt in heavy pallor, as Caligari's sleeper or as *The Man Who Laughs*. Every postcard would be on rotation at my whim. But right then, since I had yet to recover my babies in total and more were coming, I just stuck the ones I had up at random and, an hour later, walked over to the Pronto convenience store for something nutritious or fortified with over-appropriate vitamins. I could see now that this was going to be my routine, and I welcomed the steps and my stab at familiarity. The five minutes it took to get there and the five minutes it took to get back were not exercising, but there was some social expenditure in the effort. I was in the world; I could kick over a loose brick or stare down a black cat, and whenever I returned to my house, I felt like I could say I'd done something close to sweaty.

Jonah was in the shop when I got there, buying another stack of newspapers.

"Hey, Ouija," my neighbor said, and the cashier looked at me funny.

"Oh, hey, Jonah," and I stared back at the cashier until the guy pretended to be busy with the register.

"What, you here for another sack of tall boys?"

"No, man, not tonight. I'm gonna have a Gatorade or a Clamato or maybe a big bad bottle of Schweppes."

"Well, if you fall off the wagon between now and 9 p.m., stop by. I'll be watching the fight, and I've got the fridge set with lots of German and Belgium brews, plus that cheapo stuff we drank today." Of course, I went over. I mean, who did I think I was kidding with my V8 and Diet Sprite? I spent two hours trying to do what I thought was yoga on the too-cold tiles, started an exhale that turned into laughter, then rose and went over to Jonah's. I didn't know anything about boxing except that when I was a kid, I thought the fight had to be about bigger things like some country was boxing for milk, or a man needed to win back his wife and had to wear colored shorts and get punched in the face to achieve this goal. But it was cool to be hanging out with Jonah. He screamed at the set, and I felt like a part of some dumb joke that mated me to wicker dens and casinos and Hemingway and shit-faced pronouncements of injustice. Before I knew it, the match was over, and we were talking out the events at the kitchen table. There was never a lull in the conversation. "Boy, what a clown! Can you believe that mess?" Hey, I didn't know what he was talking about, but Jonah was right about the yum yum beers; they were better than what we drank earlier. It got late, and the talk spun more to the serious, the personal. "What's your deal, Ouija? You a fag or what?"

Huh?

"And if you *are* queer, shouldn't you be running with the young and shameless?"

I choked a little on my beer but swallowed and felt quick peace.

"You were you one of Brian's, right?"

"Okay, *what?*"

"You know, Brian, the guy who lived in your place before he broke the lease and ran off. He was into guys; he was into guys *and* girls and they all kind of looked like you. Some were really skinny, but they all had that hair, black, messed."

"No, I wasn't 'one of Brian's.'"

"That fucker and I could get along, the two of us could jab easy, and when he left, I even helped clean up his pad, so the landlady didn't sue his ass for what he'd done to the walls and corners, the bricks and mailbox."

"Damn."

"Hey, kid, people lived in that house before you moved in, you know: single-income families, college brats, and the occasional lonely guy with a job and just himself to look after. For years and years, an unfettered flux of new deposits, new renters." Jonah got quiet, but there seemed to be practice in the way he stretched out before saying, "I never give any thought to what any of them are or do." Jonah tried to sit straight, snaked up on his chair with terrible ease, and then added, "Everything is cool with me so long as you want whatever it is you want. That's what I told Brian when he was down. Jerking off in a room, I told him, nothing else but your desire, I said. You better crave the noise in your head, get cuddle-love with the thoughts that make you hot, the world that the rest of us do not get to see." I didn't say anything, so Jonah kept going, skating around the hot dot of whatever he needed to leap across. "Everything is a shadow before it becomes the love you can belt, the love you have to chase down and absolutely have, the love you'll hurt to get. A hole in a wall because you couldn't take the wall or Spackle over that wall because you couldn't take the hole."

Then Jonah kind of shut up. I looked down at the tiles. Jonah was drunk, and maybe everything he said was breaking his heart; maybe he was like this guy who always wondered about his chances with the world but never gave anything a shot, and saying things out loud was like reliving a life of perennial non-commitment.

"Sorry, man," I said and added, "I didn't think we were sticking to any subject. I mean you just talk and talk, right?"

Jonah looked up at me with that same half-smile, never genuinely elicited. There was a stack of complimentary fast food straws leaning against the sugar shaker. He picked one up and stood it upon itself, then pulled the white paper that sheathed it away into a squished caterpillar an object of fragility. I stared at the crimped paper and asked Jonah if he wanted a beer. He said yes, didn't say what I thought he might say, which would have been *Oh, no, man, it's too damn late,* and all that baloney that would cover up shame or guilt and would be my cue to get up and perhaps save my neighbor some embarrassment. Instead, he poured the last drop from his bottle onto the paper caterpillar. I heard myself gasp as the straw slip began to wriggle and lengthen with its saturation. I had not seen that trick since I was twelve. It made me happy, pure and done happy. I was about to stand and get Jonah another beer when he picked the wet paper straw skin off the table, put it in his mouth, and walked to the fridge.

"Christ, man, I didn't know you needed one *that* bad."

Jonah and I got smashed, drank all the beers, then the harder stuff in the cabinet, and we fell into those pools where you scream and laugh and feel like you're in big, sad trouble. The conversation was all about cop shows and hippie songs, crook presidents and dream cars, Raquel Welch and Salma Hayek. We talked about all the houses we had lived in and all the movies we wished we had never seen; we talked about all the people we no longer talked to, and we were so free to do so because, as Jonah put it, we were grown men and didn't have, "a mommydaddy or loverwife to keep us out of the jivehive." So we could get stupider and stupider until we stilled, out of exhaustion, or one of us just passed out.

But we slowed down, thank God. We drank water in between sips of whiskey, and I smoked a few of Jonah's cigarettes. As we cooled off, Jonah said, "My daughter, Shanie, is getting married."

"Wow, you've got a daughter. Is she hot?"

"She's beautiful, you cocksucker faggot."

"Must take after her mother, then."

"Sure does. My baby girl looks just like Sara, down to the heavy freckles and the eyebrows."

"Does 'baby girl' have a boyfriend?"

Jonah looked at me as if to say: *Jeez, boy, I thought you could hold it.* Then I remembered, "Oh, yeah, getting married," and I laughed like a cartoon Dracula would laugh if he had the cartoon chance. Jonah didn't laugh, but he resumed his half-smile, in wormy suspension. I loved his smile; it meant safety in his head, and I was lucky to see the expression.

"Shanie's getting married. I thought they were going to announce it last week so I bought ten papers. But it was this week that they announced it."

Jonah kept smiling, and I didn't want to say another word.

THE NEXT DAY WAS sunny and hot; it could have been beautiful, but my belly hurt from all the drinking, and I kept thinking about Jonah, his daughter and her impending wedding, his daddy, and the boss that didn't bother showing up to Jonah's barbecue. When I had finally left his place the night before, he was in good spirits, telling jokes and even ending the night with, "I hope you know I'm just talking out of my ass. I'm a fifty-five-year-old preacher's boy with an ex-wife and a sister who doesn't trust me, blames me for every bad move she's ever had with men or money. Christ, I am entitled to drunk talk, if that's all I ever get; I am entitled."

I made coffee, let the afternoon creep over before going out to the mailbox. Inside the box sat a single postcard and a gas bill from the tenant who had lived here before me. I didn't recognize the postcard. It was a Garfield the lazy orange cat postcard. I liked Garfield well enough, but there was no way I would have bought a Garfield postcard and sent it to myself. I turned it over and read: HEY, BRIAN! HOW COME YOU DON'T CALL OR COME BY? WE MAY BE OVER, BUT DON'T I STILL HAVE ALL YOUR TAPES? LOVE, LISA. I looked at the name on the gas bill: Brian English. Brian English didn't live here anymore, and he apparently hadn't bothered giving the post office or LISA a forwarding address. Brian English would never get this Garfield postcard, and he would probably never get his TAPES and what the hell could LISA do about it? I sneezed and gripped too hard on the mail. The postcard bent into an abrupt V, and the gas bill glided into the street that divided my home from Jonah's. I heard a bark, quick and over. It must have been Jonah's dog; I had never seen the pet but recalled that the name on the doggie bowl was MAW. I looked at Jonah's yard to try to see the animal, but it didn't matter if I saw it. MAW was awake, whether or not I was a witness to the fact.

They Let Me Drive

Tomás, our mail and delivery guy, had a nervous breakdown, just wasn't showing up or calling in sick, and when we got in touch with his wife she started to scream about how we pushed him bad, and now Tomás was broken. "Don't expect him to come by the store, and if he does, don't be so cruel as to hire him back." Boss and I didn't guess at what Inez meant, but Tomás was a mess anyway, always showing up too early, like he hadn't slept most of the night, bringing in coffee for everyone even though we had a coffee machine, sweating like hell when you asked him to do anything he wasn't used to, laughing like a cartoon weasel when you asked him what he did on his weekends, and never using the men's room at the store.

Right after Boss got off the phone with Inez, he turned to me and said, "I'm going to need you to do some deliveries and some easy errands. Is that cool?"

"Yeah, it's cool, but it's not what you hired me for."

"It won't be a big deal. Just take an extra two hours after lunch and drop off some packages at the UPS, then pick up some boxes at the post office. I'll give you a gas card and a nametag, and you'll be set."

"Even though I don't own a vehicle?"

"You can use the truck I issued Tomás. That mother's been watering his plants all week, and I was going to let him use the truck for a while, but then I see his boy, Jacob, cruising around in the Ford, getting burgers and parking by the high school track, steering with one hand and holding the company cell to his ear with the other, and I don't think the punk's even got a permit. So to hell with Tomás and to hell with Jacob. I'm getting that truck back tomorrow, even if I have to call that kid up on the phone I doled out to his daddy and pretend like I'm offering him his pop's old job."

I LIVE CLOSE TO the shop; the main reason I wanted to work at the pharmacy was so I could have my walk to and from making money. This errand boy routine was going to flip me all offended, but I didn't want to be like Tomás and get jitter-pissed with any proffered task. So I acquiesced like a dope, did the file and cataloguing stuff in the morning and then grabbed whatever letters or packages needed to go out that day. I am a terrific driver because I would never want to get behind the wheel on my time. I actually quit driving around the same time I quit college. Also, I've always been so afraid of the way some jerks don't look at the road or check their mirrors., so I am totally careful but never slow or hesitant behind the wheel.

Tomás's old truck had a CD player, but I only listened to four discs: one is this Muddy Waters compilation that makes me want the night all day, and the other three are from a post-punk electro outfit called New Order. It all sounds pretty old to me and gets pretty old to listen to, especially these seven minute long synthetic songs that have frog and cricket noises, but for some reason, a real live drummer. I started to listen to a news channel that was heavy on talk, very reactionary stuff, no entitlements, zero-tolerance, lack of moral fiber rants, and a nervous amount of station identification. My deliveries were cake, but if anything burned, it was all the talk radio to which I was now subjecting myself. I had dropped my initial prejudice and let myself get to know these blowhards, even laugh at what they said, the manner in which institutions and ideologies were attacked, and there was the puny thrill of listening to the caller's sloppy grievances. How could anyone do it, just call in a radio program and say, "Flat tax is a load," or, "Yes, I support what you want to say about campaign reform, but can't you lay off Medicare?'"

I was driving to the post office to buy four rolls of stamps and mail off a tube of Stoma Paste when I heard Tomás on the radio. "Hello, is this Stan Vale? Am I talking to Stan?"

"Yes, this is Stan Vale, and you are on *The Hour*. What do you got to say, friend, about love and death and the way that last caller has just confused self-serving whininess with slow wit?"

"Oh, I thought the last guy had a point."

"Yeah, the last guy *had* a point, and then he lost it."

"Uh-huh."

"And so you've recovered it?"

"Maybe."

"And what would that point be?"

"Just that the new music is so derivative, and if you like to listen to Sinatra or Celia Cruz, it makes it so difficult to get into, to even tolerate their lessers."

"Fair point, but don't stop the presses."

"Well, anyway, I just wanted to say what a good job you're doing, Stan."

"Much appreciated."

"Yeah, you know, I just lost my job, and it's been tough, but your show has been an inspiration."

"Sorry to hear that, brother, but glad to help you out, glad to be a part of your life, and really, folks, that's what *The Hour* is all about. We want to hear from you, get your take, and do whatever we can. Now, onto to Rich in Denton, Texas. Rich, you're on *The Hour*." Rich thought marijuana should be legal, and so did everyone else who called in after him. I parked the green Ford a block from the post office in the lot of an athletic shoe store so I could walk around and remember my legs.

I've never been into cars or trucks; I didn't think the Batmobile looked cool, always fought weird boredom when watching that *Transformers* cartoon, and was genuinely bothered by all the sarcasm coming from that talking *Knight Rider* car. Although in my life I have made liberal use of drive-thru banking and drive-thru take-out, the pure idea of these amenities has carried a legitimate shudder of lazy terror when I think about it. When I drive, I *never* think. I hit the brakes for stop signs and hit for red or yellow lights, never hit anyone, and get where I'm going with a feathery tact that I would be smart to extend over other areas of my life. When I'm not driving, I think of myself as some kind of progressive saint, so I don't get to feel like a hypocrite, because I never wanted to take for granted what it meant to speed up/slow down and have minutes be something other than breathing and pacing. I was not ever totally against driving, either. I mean, I always managed to get rides or use the bus, but if I could help it, I walked everywhere. To swagger or march from point to point kept me tanned and restful in mind.

But that was all going away. Besides the sense of atrophy in the calves and thighs and the pin-prick numbness under heels, the worst part of what I was doing was trying to find some of these houses. Many of our clients lived along rural routes just outside of the city. Some didn't have a phone, or we didn't have their number, and the descriptions on the delivery slip would be, "It's the yellow house; it's the white, yellow house." You got to where you thought a client lived, and all the houses were a little yellow, a little white. Even though I knew so much better, I kind of got the feeling that the clients didn't want just anyone to know where they lived, a notion which really made no proper sense, but as I drove around and couldn't find what I was looking for, my mind would creep toward inept conspiracy. It was a bit of a bummer, but so far, only a mild frustration, not like what Tomás must have suffered. Although, I think finding these houses and getting to talk to the ailing people inside was what Tomás liked best about his job.

The man used to tell the story of an elderly woman who, against the wishes of her son and caregiver, wanted to try to start moving around her house again. She wasn't crippled or in the degenerative throes of muscle disease, but since she'd received a lift chair from our company, she had stopped doing the many little things that had once been her life of motion. *Mrs. Flores called me because she said the chair we gave her stopped working, and she needed help getting up. Her son Danny took care of her. He didn't work, but he cooked meals for her and made sure she slept and looked after the plants. He was in town paying his insurance and she called to ask if I could help. I was in the area anyway. I just helped her a little. When she got on her feet, she walked straight to the kitchen.* Tomás had to stall his words; the man was always almost crying, and I had long since stopped feeling embarrassed for him. *When she got to the sink, she turned the faucet on the sponge and squeezed the water out. There were no dishes to wash. Her son kept the house clean. Mrs. Flores walked back to the chair on her own, but I held her hand as she bent her knees to sit. Man, I wish someone else could have seen it, too, how beautiful she was.*

"DID YOU HEAR TOMÁS? That crumb bum was on the radio just now, kissing butt and saying how he lost his job. He didn't *lose* his job. You know that, right? That he just stopped coming?"

"Yeah, I know that. I was here when he 'stopped coming.' I have to stand in line at the UPS and sit in traffic because he 'stopped coming.'"

Boss scratched at the left side of his belly, pulling his shirt an inch out of its tuck. "You know how long it takes to get on that show, *The Hour*? I called up once to weigh in on that water issue and hung up after thirty minutes. And I was using the office phone, didn't have to hold it to my ear. You know what? I bet Tomás is using our cell to make these calls—I'm paying for his goddamn opinions to be aired!"

My forehead was resting on a stack of manila folders that contained our billing information for the last six months. Hot breath from my nostrils curled its tickle up along the stubble on my cheeks. "Well, I don't know. Just cancel service, for Christ's sake," I kind of raised my voice then settled.

"No, no, can't. I paid for all these minutes, and you could be using that phone when you're on the road. No, I've got to just get the phone back."

THE DRIVE HOME AFTER work was too quick; I was inside and on the couch in five minutes, feeling spent and irregular. It was raining outside, and this would have been one of those days where I might have asked Tomás for a lift home anyway. I decided to drive to the Dairy Queen, and if the trip seemed too speedy, I would motor down to the Dairy Queen in the next town. I had some funny idea that there was a coupon for chicken strips in my wallet. I wasn't hungry yet because I wasn't walking anymore. I mean, where was the caloric expenditure? As I drove, I flexed my back and legs and took deep breaths; it was something.

I listened to Dr. Holly get mad at all the separated women who called her, and I listened to her talk down to a guy who said he didn't know if he was in love but always wanted to be married, and shouldn't he just force a union, be a man and stay with his off-and-on girl, commit despite his hiccups of callow reservation. Because the caller kept restating his problem and didn't listen to Dr. Holly's advice, which was "get to know yourself *first* and don't expect anyone to deal with quirks that are still being denied," she cut him off and moved on to the next caller.

"Hello, Dr. Holly, I love your program and just wanted to call and say how much it means to me that you are on the air."

"Oh, Jeez, you're embarrassing me. Well, thank you; that means lots, but did you have a question, or would you like to add to our People Poll?"

"No, I just wanted you to know you are appreciated. I just lost my job, and it's hard, but listening to your show really helps."

Then Dr. Holly started to grill Tomás: What happened at work? Why were you let go? How is your family coping? Are you actively looking for new employment, or do you call up radio help and think that is life?

"We're doing okay. My wife works, and we have some money saved. My son's got a weekend job, and we hurt for nothing."

"So what did you used to do?"

"They let me drive."

I was hungry now, hungry enough to forget about the coupon that was maybe in my wallet and just buy a combo meal at the closest place I could find, a burger joint that was trying to push some lottery prize on its customers. If I was going to keep driving, I was going to have to renew my license, which was something I dreaded. It wasn't the written test or the line at the DMV that brought me down, but a kind of vanity. My old license looked good; somehow my hair and smile came off with real zest and potential, and I can look at that person and wonder at all the lost fun. I wouldn't be able to take that kind of shot again. Maybe it was just something gone from the eyes. I could go for handsome—wear nice clothes and cut my hair like some guy in a magazine—but never just be the messy, fun boy in a T-shirt and smirk, and that made me feel polluted, desperate, and yearning for the kind of stasis achieved only in motion.

"What, did you sleep in your shirt last night?"

"Yeah, and I fucked in it, too."

Boss laughed. Who knows if he believed me.

"Hey, stallion, before you go off and claim the lame, take this," and he placed Tomás's cell phone on the counter.

"Wow, you got it back. Did he put up a fight or did he—?"

"No, man, Tomás was civil. In fact, we talked it out, and he might even come back to the store. He needs to work or else he's got nothing but his time. He needs to get tired and feel worn."

"And driving wasn't doing that for him?"

Boss was quiet, then said, "Tomás wants to do what you do. I told him I would ask you first, but he wants to know if you could take over the deliveries full time, and let him do the filing and ordering and learn the computer. I've known Tomás for fifteen years. I can't afford to hire anyone new, but if it helps you decide, I can offer you a raise."

DRIVING BACK FROM THE pharmacy, I messed with the dial. There was a lot of talk even on the rock stations, and I wanted to avoid it all, but I couldn't take an afternoon of street silence either. Between a Big Band station and NPR was a net of crinkling, sizzling static. I turned the textured-nothing up so that it filled the inside of the truck. I didn't know what I would eat at home or if I would go out; I just wasn't hungry yet, and I understood that my appetite would be all up and down and far from stable for weeks to come. Then, I might find a hearty rhythm. Then, I might never welcome its arrhythmia.

As I turned onto my street, I saw Tomás's boy, Jacob, walking back from school, walking with a girl, holding hands. The kid looked nothing like his father. He was all Inez—that worry in the eyes and forehead and that super black hair—but maybe he was wearing his dad's old work shirt. If I hadn't taken over this job, maybe he'd be driving this truck with his girl in the passenger seat. I passed the young couple, then slowed down, tried to see what they looked like—if they were beautiful—in the rearview mirror. The girl was looking down at her steps, then at the houses to her right. Jacob recognized the vehicle he used to drive around before his daddy snapped, was watching the truck slow down, looking at the license plate, and then he met my eyes in the rearview mirror. I revved up to a go speed and drove past my house. I didn't want to be home right then, and now that I knew the kids were beautiful, I didn't want them to know where I lived.

Ruby Coast

Before he was on five hundred stations and you either loved or wanted to hurt him for the swing of his on-air strife, I knew the man. That's most of his birth certificate name; lots of these radio guys get a flashy fake one, but "Ruby Coast" was flashy fake enough. His complete name, before he cut it up for the AM smooth, was Ruben Costigan. I was too young to be his best friend or his poker buddy. All I knew for sure about this guy was that he had a good-looking wife who taught Spanish at my high school. She had a luxuriant mane of red-brown hair that I knew was a dye job, a tan that I knew was from a booth, and she made a face like everything was way too serious and heavy to think about. When I let myself check her out, I, of course, thought she was too good for him. Maybe she knew this and maybe she didn't, but she never hesitated to treat Ruben like the bum the rest of us down the street thought he was. The couple made vile noise for the people who had to live next door, but whatever broken dishes and banshee screaming occurred, I always knew it was all Ruben's fault; it had to be him. Ruben was at fault way before he hooked up with Resa. He already had two divorces and the man was twenty-seven.

Ruben was a fat guy behind the mic even then, but in those days, he was always fighting his bulk—off sugar for a week, taking up cigarettes, hoping for a metabolic jumpstart. You could see him jogging and want to laugh your ass off. Really, he was only a mess in life. If you heard him do commercials for the local tax agencies or pool joints, he came off as a different man: authoritative, exact, and never overaggressive. He could sell you your own lawn chairs, and he was quick with his on/off cool button. When I knew Ruben, he was in trouble, done with the local DJ stint, and suing his boss for wrongful termination. His wife, Resa, had gone, and she was the big paycheck, it turned out. He was the guy who had to clip coupons, exhaust his credit cards, and make the frozen dinners last.

I was sixteen and used to mow down his lawn for ten or fifteen dollars. If he owed me a couple of bucks, I'd be nice and let the debt slide. Sometimes we got his mail by accident. One day, there was a stack of important-looking letters in our box, and when I brought it to his door, the guy looked like he was going to faint.

White-faced, spanking his neck with cupped fingers, he beckoned "Come in, come in, man. Don't slam the door. Come in." I came in because Ruben looked like he was going to collapse and go to dust over the welcome mat. Ruben was okay enough to swagger-stand, then walk over to a margarine-yellow desk lamp to examine the return address. "It's the wife or the wife's lawyer. She wants more. I always asked her what she wanted, and it was always *more*. I like this house, and she says it's a good starter home. I get her this ring, and she makes a face but wears it anyway. I'm not going to tell you to never get married. When it works, you are a blessed animal, but then you can feel endangered, and you get that panic like you're the last of your kind, the last of your*self*, even. Oh, God, don't listen to me."

Ruben had his habits back then. They were real, and they were threatening, but they were not why his wife left him, not why he got fired from his afternoon drive-time gig. The man was a functioning *every*thing, was good at deadlines and alarm clocks, and writing up quick proposals. He smoked, drank, snorted, and popped pills, and the man could eat like it was a contest to win more recuperative sleep. Right then, I had come to his door while he was trying to kick. That's why he looked transparent and itchy with some bad ghost under the skin.

"Do me a fav, bro. Check on me. Tonight at six, then, if I'm okay, maybe check on me at nine."

"Are you sure you don't want me to call an ambulance?"

"No, that's cool, but if I'm okay at nine, maybe you could call me up at eleven."

I didn't come by, but I called at ten—eight rings and no answer. I called again and heard that click and dead line hum as if someone had kicked the phone off its stand.

I told myself this wasn't my problem and slept well, probably dreamt of cars and girls; back then I usually didn't recall dreams and would just wake in a healthy shock of consciousness wanting only to shower and eat. Three days later, I stopped by his house. Now Ruben Costigan was beaming, no longer dumpling pale but pork rose. "I'm off it all except for cigarettes and a little Jack on ice to cool me down. But for now, I'm good for the move."

Ruben was more sober than not, and how did he kick? He told himself that others had done far worse, *far* worse, and survived, even thrived. He knew it would be counter-life to tell himself that an equal many had done far less and not come through. Ruben kept thinking of all the men who held up the VFW and somehow kept their homes and wives. He hugged himself like there would never be anybody else. Maybe this got him started on his personal politics, whatever self-reliance he gets paid to publicly espouse. Ruby Coast makes his money doing the pundit's sulk and scream, but he's no static clown. He swirls his position to show off; he bends like hell to be the right man, as if his three hours are a con job employing the most pointed, restricted jazz. This is an art, no doubt, and he knows he might be the best at kicking its aesthetics around for the uninitiated.

When I decided to check on him, he had cleaned himself up. Ruben didn't look good; he never looked good, but for the first time ever, he looked like he held purpose, and you could see that he was dressing for some intended target—tan slacks and a beige tie, after-shave accenting his perspiration.

"Sorry I didn't stop by when you asked."

He shook his head and walked over to fish his hand in a candy jar of toffee and Tootsie Rolls. The guy kept candy all over the house: Starburst, Almond Joy, Skittles. Right then, when he opened the door for me, he was chewing on a Sugar Daddy. "It was better for me that you didn't show. I even yanked the cord out of the wall so I wouldn't call Resa or my sister. I just told myself that was all. No more."

"And now you're okay? You're better?"

"Doesn't matter if I'm better. I'm gone."

Ruben Costigan was letting go of his world, which was nothing now that Resa was out of the picture. He had no children, and, "Fuck her cats." He was prepared, inflamed, poised for the big pounce. There were other jobs, other women, "other cities, over and over, until the big until," and then—as if a malignant spirit wanted to punctuate this observation—a rock hit the window. Ruben flinched but went on, "You must claim what is yours, what is out there for you. Don't expect any help because what's out there is all that we get." Another rock hit the window behind him, this time shattering glass and sliding down the mini-blinds to thud on the carpet.

"Man, who hates you so much?"

"Those kids in Resa's class. You probably know some of them. Stupid punks. They loved her for nothing because she was beautiful and acted like she didn't know, and there is *no way* I could've treated her right in their eyes. I'm the bad guy. They want to kill me."

"No, they don't, man. They just want to be terrible, and you're easy to poke at."

"Yeah."

He was out of the house that night. We never really said bye. He tried to give me a twenty to even out whatever he might have owed me for his lawn work, but he couldn't find or wouldn't let go of the bill. He pulled twelve singles from his pockets and gave them to me in his handshake.

When I walked out of his place, I noticed key markings all along the sides of his cobalt Camaro. HERS. HERS. PRICK. HERS. He left the convertible there. Resa never came back for it, and as the months turned, nobody claimed the vehicle, and I got to watch rust seize over its exterior. The next time Resa, or any of us, knew anything about her husband, he was "Ruby Coast," same guy she married but now in quotes that bound a truncated form of his name. Whatever anyone has to say about how he defends all policy, and decries nearly every entitlement, the guy is just amazing. Ruby does commercials for softness-adjustable beds and holiday teddy bears. He's good at the sales pitch, and his comedic scat is even entertaining in a way. He wins arguments all the time by choosing not to argue, by just letting the caller go nuts or praise him. It sounds easy—inevitable when you hear him—but you know that means it has to be work. He can be funny. He can even get me to wait out the Amber Alerts. I know he's just a devil in this game, his talent so stitched to that radio world, so sewn that he can't do anything else. Ruby Coast looks guilty on television, and you wouldn't want to see him on film, but he had a cable show for two minutes, and his autobiography has been optioned.

I listen to him in the car; I'm usually not embarrassed to be listening. When, after sloshing about for more than the typical number of college years and staying away from the town I grew up in, I was ready to stay with my parents for a while and try to find some work, I made sure to listen to his show on the drive down. Pulling into my folks' driveway, I saw Resa back at her old house. The same kind of hair and tan, that's how I knew her. Her legs had thickened under the nylon, and I wasn't able to recognize her right off, except for her style and the pinched look in her eyes that always made me think she could be a model. She was trying to hold up a stack of papers on her knee and lock the door to her sedan. When I saw her, when I knew it was her, I lowered the volume way down, parked my truck, and didn't wave hi or anything.

Ruby Coast never talks about his personal life, if he has dogs or if he hates cats. I've never heard him say a word about Resa, her name or occupation, or how she might have skipped him toward this destiny. Here's what people know He's been married three times. He accepted welfare for seven "embarrassing months," right when I knew him probably, right before Resa took off. Ruby Coast says he understands Jesus Christ, and Jesus Christ was no Socialist, even though the actual gospels hint otherwise. Ruby gets in trouble. I mean, he shoots his mouth off for a living, and sometimes that doesn't go so well. So when everyone thinks he's a misogynist or a bigot, and I know he's just quick and sarcastic, there is something like sympathy in me, but I don't know where to place this leniency. Ruby Coast can't believe all that he says about borders and war bonds, about jails and the IRS. No goddamn way. Unless he does, unless he really, really does, and then I have nothing to say. I listen to him though; everyone does, as he lends his blessing to a candidate, as he offers NASA his Valentine's Day commentary, and derides his goofy conspiracy late night radio competition: "Looks like I'm all alone here. I go on these sites that these hosts talk about, where there is speculation about diamonds on the moons of Jupiter or Mars. This is just me folks, but can you *think* of anything *less* romantic?"

Open House

I'd spent all that week mowing down the grass behind a Home Depot and pulling rotten planks off a torn-down one-hour photo lab. Back from this landscaping-demo work, out of my grey-green truck, and walking the dehydrated zombie walk to get to my kitchen faucet, I heard this out-of-control laughing, these out-of-breath, spontaneous joy noises. My across-the-street neighbor—a thin girl with puff-bleached hair who looked about twenty or twenty-one—was run-jumping over a defaced *For Sale* sign that had been hammered into the lawn for over two months. She kept making the shy leap and screaming out as she tumbled to the dying grass, whereupon this lanky crew cut high school kid would walk up to and step over the sign in a single exaggerated maneuver. My neighbor would again jump the sign, and the guy would try to take pictures with what I took to be a disposable camera.

I got inside and cracked loose a plastic tray of ice cubes into a large, clean salad bowl on the counter, filling the bowl with tap water. After slurping down for twenty seconds, I pushed my face into the bowl like a dog. When most of the water had poured out, I lifted the bowl up so that what was left fell over my chest and the ice spun toward the drain.

The house I rented had a screened porch built around the front door; that's where I would recline to rest after any sweat work and accept the way the day had gone down. I'd lie there by the breeze or the no-breeze, and whatever I had to do would slink away in flags of abiding recession. I could see out of the screen mesh and believe that no one could see their way in. I rested my head on the comparably cool cement behind the porch screen, damp in this dusky shade. Privacy clung to me and helped me do everything else.

The young people were still outside. I could hear them start to get tired and, after playing, they took their healthy, hapless mirth indoors.

The next day was planting baby trees and bright-thistled flowers along the pecan-shell-covered alley of a children's museum. The generous man I worked with (really, the generous man I worked *for*) had come to realize that the weedwacker and the leaf-blower were making nothing easier for me. I excelled at wielding the machete and was decent at raking. Put a hat and some sunscreen on me, and I could go all day. We came to agree that I would toil with the hand tools, and he would touch-up the sidewalk edges, as well as do the spinning motor work he felt was way easy and which I felt was too much. I was getting six before-taxes bucks an hour, and if I thought of this clock-in wage, I would feel oppressed and exploited, but if I just thought of this work as a kind of physical exercise that I got paid to perform, then that made me feel okay, if not ecstatic about the way I made my money.

It started sprinkle-raining on the worksite, and the boss didn't want to chance messing up the blades, so I was home earlier than usual. After I took a shower and stepped into clean, soft clothes, I walked over to knock on my neighbor's door.

My neighbor opened up wearing a pair of nerdy black glasses and had flour or paste on her cheeks and overalls. She greeted me with due civility, looked busy but glad to break away from her indoor task. I heard myself speaking to her as if from another room.

"I saw the *by Owner* sign—Hi, I'm your neighbor, Ernesto—I saw the sign and wanted to ask about the house."

"This is my uncle's place. I rent from him. My name is Lee. Yeah, it's a good place, right by my school, and the man won't sell to me because he doesn't think I'd make the payments."

"Is it open for walk-ins?"

Lee tilted her head to the side as if to see which direction I'd walked from. "You live next door, Ernesto?"

"Yeah, *right* next door. I feel like such a dolt for not coming by earlier, just to introduce myself and be a good person."

"Like I say, this place is not mine," Lee started to thumb at the powder specks on her forehead, "so I don't feel any special obligation to dress it up for a walk around, but you can check it out, see the rooms, see the outside yard."

As Lee walked me from kitchen to bedroom, I realized all the mess on her was from a papery collage-structure she was detailing in the living room, or the large floor space that the architect had supposed would be a living room. Lee used the area as a work spot "for these easily-ruined installations" of hers. Lee waved her right arm before a semi-circle of white and blue papier-mâché flower pots that had been blow-torched, soaked with aquamarine tempera sponge marks, and stuck all over with candy wrappers. I didn't say I liked them because I didn't feel I could contextualize an appreciation enough to like them but, as I wasn't ready for the display and even felt mild shock, my silence was sincere. We walked past the laundry room, on toward the backyard. The grass was dry, and the earth that showed beneath looked scorched. There was a sleeping bag rolled atop an old realtor sales sign and a half-dozen amber-hued ashtrays staked into each other atop a water-damaged telephone directory.

"I don't know what Abe is asking. I can give you his number, but if you're for real about buying, wait until Friday, so I can move my things into my boyfriend's place."

In my place that night, I felt a comfort I had not known since moving to this address. I liked the property enough to sign the lease and think I might even re-sign, but I wasn't used to the house, and I kept thinking that maybe I didn't ever want to get used to being there, which was perhaps why I really liked to stay in that porch area and feel as if that was how I connected to this block. I enjoyed knowing that Lee was here, knowing that she had a place to stay, and that she had a boyfriend who had an apartment in which she could move her belongings. At night, that boyfriend came over, and the two would do this fake-looking karate in the yard. They would leap and leap over that *by Owner* sign and laugh, and the guy would spin a kick-block and cry out in comedic warrior call.

I was watching TV, a public access show about restoring sailboats. In the other room, I had the radio on, a commercial program about selling manufactured houses. In the kitchen, the dishwasher was going. I was waiting something out, pushing back a true world. I was trying to blanket some noise, wanted to be sacked by some hush of time.

In the morning, after I made my call to Lawn Gone and found out where I would be meeting my boss for a few hours of weed-work and my Friday check, I saw what looked like a destroyed piñata over my neighbor's mailbox. Lee's yellow Thunderbird wasn't there, and the curtains were drawn in a manner that looked ordered and different. I started walking to my truck and realized that the busted piñata by the mailbox was actually one of the collage sculptures I had seen the day before, placed out for a garbage collection that was running late.

I adopted a spectral involvement at Lawn Gone. I did everything I was told but refrained from asking if there was more to be done, never added my speculation about the project, and the boss let me alone; he drove off the site to run other errands, brought me a barbecue sandwich sack lunch and a Big Gulp of iced tea when he met me on the grass, and told me that I was the second or third best guy he'd ever worked with. He paid me my week's money in an envelope of tens and twenties. I thought I was getting a check, but he thought this would be better for the both of us; getting actual cash kind of *was* better, but it also separated me from a feeling of that taxable exchange, of dreaming scheming capitulate banking.

"Thanks, man. Let me know if you need me next week."

"Oh, I will *for sure* need you next week. You let *me* know when you want to work." I could not trust myself to do so. The work—aside from the flattery that was supposed to make me think I should make a career out of this part-time experience with Lawn Gone—was thirsty and fairly thankless. I was qualified for really anything else, and that knowledge was starting to pick at me.

Back home, there was a new car in Lee's driveway, a suds-and-cream-colored convertible with the coal-grey top up. The piñata-looking sculpture had been removed by the trash men, and the driveway had been watered down.

Working the way I had worked today, not over-concerned about impressing my employer but somehow still impressing the man, there was less sweat on me, less dirt. I looked like I had been playing around in the world for fun, kicking a soccer ball or running alongside a bicyclist, not yanking at weeds with garden gloves in that one pair of jeans I didn't mind ruining. The door was open, and there was a robust fellow who resembled a paler, pinker-faced Smokey Robinson in a white sports coat and jeans, whisper-nodding negatives into a cellular phone in the crook of his neck. The man turned to look at me when I got to the door, excused himself to the person he was talking to, and squinted down his eyes to see me better as he pitched the tiny phone into a coat pocket.

"Is this an open house yet?"

"This house has been open for a month, but the occupant wouldn't make that easy or known."

"Ah, Lee?"

"You know my niece, huh? You're not that boyfriend of hers, are you?"

"I think I may be out of the age range for that job."

"You'd *think* so, but you didn't see the last guy—Telly Savalas at his primetime peak."

"I don't actually know your niece. I mean, I just met her. I was asking about the house last week. Lee was good enough to give me a tour."

The man made a diffident face, sore and slick with insider news. "This house is not *ready* for a tour. Not until there is a paint job, a spray job, and a twice-over, and I've got to bring in the drapes and shelves she was supposed to find for me. Lee was supposed to set it up, but all she did was make that trash." The man pointed down and waved his arms at the living room floor where Lee's collage-sculpt work had been.

"Those display pieces?"

"That last guy—the old-as-me, turtleneck baldy, way-older-than-you guy—he taught art at the college up the road. I think he must have encouraged her. Lee changed her major and everything. but that's something my niece *would* do. She goes Business, then she goes Psychology; she never thinks that one could be a minor, and then she's making cardboard boxes with plaster and the funny pages. What do you do for a living, my man?"

"All this week, I've been cutting grass. And planting."

The homeowner smiled and said, "My name is Abraham. You live across the street?"

"Correct. I rent."

"You like this block?"

"Yeah, it's nice. I mean, since your niece left, I'm the loudest one here, and I am not loud."

"And your lease is close to up?"

"My lease is—"

"Look, I'll give a guy like you fifty bucks a day for cleaning this place up and being here when someone comes by to peruse."

I didn't say anything.

"Sounds like you do a lot of temp work, am I right?"

"Right now, yeah, for sure."

"Okay, well, you can pretty much work from home—your home, my home—and keep up this lawn. You can crash here any night; I'd actually prefer that. Make sure you show people around when someone wants to see the house until I sell this place. You clean up the property, water the grass, and people will be interested. Then you show them around and let me know who has come by. You can even size them up for me."

I put my thumb to the stubble on my chin as if thinking it over, started to chew on my index fingernail, realized I had made up my mind and then wondered what, if anything, I could glean from hiding that information.

"Look—what's your name?"

"Ernesto, or Ernie."

"*Or Ernie*, I'm going to hire someone for this, maybe a kid from this neighborhood, but I'd rather hire a man. You want the job, call me tomorrow, and we'll talk it out. That niece of mine was keeping people away. You just have to let those same curious people be."

I didn't jump to get the job right off. I waited for the day to be its own enterprising flower, waited for hunger and the pull of a naptime because that kind of waiting made me feel like I was in control. I called up Abraham and said that if he needed someone to look after the house, I'd be the guy to keep the property clean and fleckless for any interested party. Abraham was glad I'd come around, but it didn't turn out to be that fifty dollars a day he initially offered. Abe would pay me for a work week, two-fifty, and then Saturday and Sunday off, unless I wanted to water the grass, check the mailbox, or take any flyers off the front door. I could, of course, sleep there on these nights as well. I could get in through the sliding glass door in the back; he said he would mail me a set of keys in two or three days.

As soon as I checked out the place, I felt a comfort roll over me so sudden and genuine that I let myself stay longer and finally lie down to sleep. There were fold-out chairs and TV trays and a computer system, all the kitchen supplies out and shiny, and a fragrance like cedar chips and cinnamon spritz-pumped into the air. This wasn't how Lee had the place when I first came in; this was Abraham's idea of a selling look and mood. It was like a brochure of middle class prosperity that reminded me of my mother's *Good Housekeeping* magazines, the decor like a studio set. It also reminded me of the interior design of the Ted Knight situation comedy, *Too Close for Comfort*. Here was the smell of closed-door air circulating, the hum of reliable appliances, and the comfy alliances of energy and asbestos in the walls. The television worked, the cable was paid for, and the stereo was set to a talk radio station that did a *drive to* show and a *drive from* show, then a conspiracy talk show went on and would rebroadcast until dawn. I would get up at odd moments all night, thinking I heard cats or midnight street marchers, and then I'd play with the dial to get a taste of all gripes and unwarranted praise. As I woke the next day, groggy from the back and forth of the new environs, I vacuumed, walked outside, lifted a wet newspaper from the lawn, went out the sliding door, and walked across the street to my place.

The second night I stayed there. The first week into the job, already feeling sneaky yet secure about this boon position, I slept on a burnt orange, too-plush couch that Abraham brought in to make the place look homey. I helped him haul the couch in; it wasn't a heavy piece of furniture, but the thing was cumbersome. Abraham had just paid twenty dollars for it at a thrift shop and didn't want to drag it on the newly-mopped linoleum tiles. As we set the couch down, Abe asked if Lee had come by the place at all.

"No, not that I've noticed, but I've been doing other things, you know."

"She still has those keys to get in. She needs to mail those keys back to me already."

"And you need to get me a duplicate set. This sliding door business is making me feel like a daylight criminal."

Abraham sat on the couch and dotted at his forehead with a handkerchief he'd pulled from the inner pocket of a teal-colored coat. "I used to help her mama, my baby sister, with that girl. Not just with groceries and extra cash. Lee's dad wasn't around then, and I would go to those teacher-parent conferences in his lousy stead. Lee was eight, and the classroom would be decorated with all these story drawings that the kids put together to show how they understood what the White House was or where a frog could live. I could spot the pictures Lee did right away. She never signed her name at the bottom of the paper like most of the third-graders, but she'd somehow work her name into the actual drawings, the letters of her name mixed up with a Marks-a-Lot castle, some Crayola fence."

"So she's always been creative?"

"I don't know about *that*, but my niece has always known who she is. Lee didn't have to pay rent here, you know. I told her to just set the place up for me like I'm now telling you to, but she insisted on giving me something, and that made her feel like she didn't have to do what I told her to do with the decorations and the grass outside. I don't need a row of tomatoes. I need the goddamned lawn watered."

I remembered and explained to Abraham that for at least two weeks now, the city had put strict water rationing into effect.

"Yeah, yeah, we've been warned before, but I don't live here right now, and they can't tie any of that mess to you, so spray away. That lawn needs to look nice in the way this whole place is looking nice. With the couch and the way you raked up that backyard debris, this house is going to sell."

Sometime after I'd nodded off, I woke to a tap-hammering sound coming from outside. I hadn't planned on sleeping on that burnt-orange couch, and as I awoke to the noise of the tapping, I was surprised that I had. I walked to the kitchen window and peered out to spy on the sound and saw Lee's boyfriend with the new *For Sale* sign that Abraham had felt the need to plant into the ground. My first impulse was to knock on the glass and holler out a threat, but I felt frozen there and had no secondary instinct to intrude upon what I was witnessing. The motion sensitive lights were already on, and the teenager was not bothered enough to stop what he was doing. My watch said it was one in the morning. In muddled fascination, I looked on as the kid tapped a new sign into the lawn, hoisted the one Abraham had just bought under his arm, and walked off. I went back to sleep without fear or guilt or concern.

In the morning, I saw the sign was not a prank or a threat, but an eager improvement over the sign Abe had just purchased and driven into the lawn; it was a bright and bold-lettered advertisement with red numbers to call. The phone number wasn't Abe's cell or the landline to this house. Back at my place, sitting on the porch to wait for the mail, I had a direct view of the number and didn't think twice about calling up and inquiring.

I heard this male voice say, "Friend-*Lee* Properties, may I help you?" I figured it was Lee's guy.

"Yeah, hi, I am wondering about a sign I saw on 8th Street and Hibiscus."

"Yeah, blue house, it's terrific, huh? You're the third call today."

"I was wondering if I might be able to view the inside. I am in the market for a home that is near the college, and this place just caught my eye."

"Ah, yeah, would you hold on for a second, just a second while I get someone, the right person you need to talk to about this?"

"No prob." I waited for close to three minutes while I heard the scuffed sound of hands palming over the receiver. Then a woman's voice came on, curt, authoritative.

"Hello, may I help you?" That got me panicky and I wanted to hang up; instead, I repeated myself.

"Yes, we can arrange a viewing. Yes, we can set one up right now. I'd like to speak to the owner then, I'll get right back to you."

She asked for my name, and I gave her my middle name. She asked for my number, and I gave her the one that was no longer in service. I said I'd call back, and the next day, I got to Abraham's house early and was prepared to be there all day, waiting for who the heck knew what. I hadn't, while I faked being an interested potential homebuyer, told Lee that I would be swinging by the property, but I got the feeling that she didn't care. She was inspired now and was going to get this place ready for the show.

At 2:32 p.m., Lee opened the door and walked right up to the line of matted pictures on the wall. Abe had pulled apart an out-of-date Expressionist calendar and had cheaply framed the Pissarro photo-reproductions along the hall and over the ugly couch.

"Yeesh," Lee said, not knowing I was in the restroom combing my hair down with water for the fourth time that afternoon. "The man used diploma frames."

"Hey," I called out.

"Abe?" Lee asked back.

I walked out to meet the situation.

"*Ernesto?*"

"Hello, Lee."

"Did you like, buy this place?"

"Not at all. Your uncle asked me to look after it, get the rooms cleaned up for an open house. I came by last week, but you weren't here."

Lee started to rub at her temples and walk around to the kitchen area. She looked older than the last time I saw her, the glamour trick of sophistication that is tied to dress and posture. She looked maybe twenty-five.

"Abe is paying you?"

"Yes."

"Is my uncle paying you good?"

"It's a little more than what I got working for Lawn Gone."

"Wow. I guess I thought there was still a shot; I thought I was still slugging for the man. I told Abe I'd clear out my clothes and books and amplifiers so he could dress the place up for walk-ins, but, you know, I thought I was still some way tied in."

"Was that your boyfriend I saw pushing down that sign?"

"Toby, yeah. He's not really my boyfriend; I say that he is or I say that

I have a boyfriend to a guy I don't know, but I *am* crashing at his pad." Lee looked around at the faux-wood paneling and plum-hued drapes that Abraham had installed and sighed. "I'm kind of thinking, I *was* kind of thinking—if I could get the buyer, do the credit checks myself, and deal with the banks—that this could be the first house I sold and if I was good at it, then this might be what I do. I know there is a license you're supposed to get, but I need to sell a house first if I want this to be what I do. I wanted this place to be the one. I never even told Abe that. I just put on like it was all his deal and I was just watching the place for him, but then I think I started to wear him out. I'm not in school anymore. He doesn't know that about me either."

Lee was looking around at the way Abe had set up the room, "Man, he put a lot of little shelves everywhere. Keep everything up high, right? But for who?"

"And this might upset a person who prefers to keep 'easily ruined installations' on the floor?"

Lee looked at me with uncertainty, but an uncertainty not bound by an unfriendly countenance.

"You don't sculpt anymore?" I asked because I wanted to know, and I would probably never be able to ask her anything again.

"Oh, I *never* sculpted. This creep in the art department was going to set me up with a show. I sometimes take pictures, like photojournalism but not attached to any text to word it up. If I *have* a thing, then *that's* my thing. Those pots that you saw, that was just me making fun of sculpting. But then I started to think that was mean, and that was already too much time."

Lee walked over to the toaster and looked at a warped reflection of her young face in its metal. "This place looks good, Ernesto, clean and good. You can tell Abe I came by if you like."

Lee started to walk toward the door, and I moved to open it for her. As she stood before the porch, Lee unlinked a set of keys from a key chain loop and handed them to me. "Front door, back gate; I'm sure you don't need them, but here."

Walking toward her yellow Thunderbird, Lee paused before the *For Sale* sign. She put her foot atop the sign and shook it back and forth until the sign loosened and hung over so that the numbers were no longer visible to anyone driving through.

"I'll tell Abe you came by," I called out from the doorway as she got into her car. Lee honked the horn twice as if to signal she heard me, then pulled away.

I closed the door behind me and stood to wait for the mail. I had seen the mail carrier coast by earlier, but he hadn't stopped at my house or this house, and I'd been here a week now and was expecting my check. I had no doubts I would get the money, but days were passing, and Abraham had not yet sent me the keys to this house. I was going to have to call him and remind him. I could use the keys his niece gave me, but I had yet to receive any compensation for this work and didn't think I was getting paid for that kind of decision-making.

The Applications

I had a job I went to two times a week. I would aid in the recreation of people who did not know it was odd if they talked about X-Men or tater tots or their dead goldfish to people they just met at the supermarket or in line at the movies. I went bowling with a seventeen-year-old girl who had been in a car wreck and was now moving about, relearning for pedestrian application the dance and pivot of motor skills once taken for granted when she was a strutter in high school. I helped a retired Navy guy organize his tool shed. I went to the movies with a boy of eleven who had not spoken since his father's accidental prescription overdose.

I was easing out of another job that was very similar, as a rec-person at an alz-home. This had been my favorite work for about six months, making the fun times happen for the high-level dementia population, and then everyone started dying all at once. Five people in a month. I heard the rattle from beds and sofas, and everyone still trying to have that good time: bingo day, chocolate day, spring-in-fall day, balloon volleyball day; it was a farce, and it was wearing me out.

THERE WAS THIS LIQUOR store I used to frequent and buy pricey beer, or if Jean wanted a hot toddy, I would go get whiskey and just drink the rest myself. Over the years, I had always kept drinking, but I lowered the habit to a steady amount of wine or lager now, and only had the hard stuff every once in a while. As I drove back from this six-hour outing with Denny—we'd gone to a kite museum, walked the turtle park, and then gotten snow cones—I saw a HELP WANTED sign on that liquor store. This place never needed help; I imagined there was a line of alkies functional enough to work the register, take their job home with them, and be back by eleven in the morning.

I thought about this idea I'd had while eating a late breakfast with Jean. She had been coming home with a lot of candles and aromatherapy trinkets, and she got free books in the mail all the time. She worked a few hours at a tourist shop, and she did some review work for an online literary journal.

"TV people say: Do what you love, and you'll be happy and make it alright," I said. "But outside of any happiness, whatever you do is really the free stuff you get, yeah?"

Jean ordered me a coffee and two potato-and-chorizo tacos because the waitress was there and Jean knew what I wanted, and I would not be able to say anything if I was in mid-riff.

"So you want cars to drive, sell cars—or like travel agents used to be. Pets supplies, pet stores. You get these candles, and you love candles, you love to have candles in your house, and so your job is a way to have that happen."

I am never so logical when I speak. That actually helps with the spontaneous points of my work, when I have to, say, negotiate a walker away from a resident approaching the dinner table. But as I drink my first four cups of coffee, I relax. The waitress put down my coffee in a Styrofoam cup and walked off to wipe down a table.

"Guess they're super busy today—out of the regular mugs," I said, something I should have realized that walking in because the place was so crowded—happy families, happy friends, hungover happies, and me, the saddest one there maybe, because I couldn't decide on getting out of my job and talking about Jean's job even on a day we were both off, still happy. And Jean was always more manageably when she was happy.

"So what 'free thing' have you received by working for a year with the senile?" she asked.

I thought about this after dropping off Denny, who had just stopped stuttering and could now get sentences out in a sure fragmentation, at his place. I drove to the liquor store that never has a HELP WANTED sign up but now does, and I pulled in, said hi to the girl that was working the register, walked over to the expensive beers, and purchased a brand I could have bought at the very convenient store two blocks from our home.

AT MY OTHER JOB, there was all of this tension because the hours were being slashed across the board. Aside from the managers and the six shift leaders, everyone was going to be cut back, including me, even though I had been given three tiny, quarter-sized raises, was complimented often, and had never been written up.

"They're going to just phase out activities, have it all be caregivers and volunteers," Pamela, a forty-seven-year-old woman who had two degrees in disciplines so impractical they required further degrees of discipline in order to be useful, said while smoking outside the building. "It's this secret, why no one will look us in the eye."

"People look me in the eye. And they smile."

"These shift leaders know something, and they are keeping it back. I need this job." Pamela was under the impression that I did not. "I live paycheck to paycheck—my divorce and my mother and my dog. I am broke now and need to have that money."

Inside the building, the residents were sitting in front of a TV set that was showing a bowling tournament. We couldn't find the remote, so that was what we watched until dinner. Dinner was tuna salad and a Nilla wafer pudding; budgets were being cut on all levels. I had stopped eating at work, and eating at work was one of the initial perks. Now I felt like we were trying to get these people to hurry up and have a heart attack or a stroke or an allergy to some additive in the fake salt. We fed them snacks all day. We let them sleep all day. We drugged them and would try to rouse them when their families came by to visit. This was not abuse. This was what you did with these residents at endgame.

"Pam, I saw a sign at this liquor store by my house. They never have a sign-up. They are open from 11 a.m. to 9 p.m., so the hours would be essentially the same. You can use me as a reference."

DENNY HAD A CRUSH on a girl at his school. "Tell me about her, man."

"Her eyes are always closed. She looks like she is walking and can see right out of closed eyes, and she never bumps the wall and never misses a chair, and when she raises her hand, I look to see her eyes, and they are still closed."

"Do you ever talk to her?"

"No."

"Does anyone talk to her?"

"She sits with two other girls."

"Talk to one of them. Tell one of them what a good time you had at putt-putt with me. Invite one of them to putt-putt. See where that takes you."

"I didn't have that much fun today. Can I tell her about the time we went looking for work?"

It had been a free day; we had no strict activity agenda, just Denny and me for about six hours, walking from shop to shop, and I would explain what I could about where we were and what each establishment did. This place sells flowers and makes its money two times a year. This place will repair tires. This place was a bakery, and it is now closed. Any time there was a HELP WANTED sign, I walked in and asked for an application, while the boy watched from the sidewalk. Denny was going to have to do this someday, and I wanted him to see the process.

"Yeah, tell about that, about how you are looking for employment. I don't think that could ever hurt."

I STOPPED AT THE liquor store to grab a bottle of mid-priced Pinot Gris. Jean was off tonight and would have made something to eat, and our favorite show *Oso* was on, so we were going to watch it as we sat on the bed drinking the wine, talking, and then sleeping. *Oso* was an over-extended miniseries about a detective who collected stamps that reminded him of his first wife; who knew how long it would run? Jean and I tried not to miss an episode. This was the new paradise I had rediscovered in our long engagement. To be tired with someone with whom you were familiar was a pleasure. The girl at the register asked to see my ID.

"Are you kidding? I come here all the time."

"Well, I've never seen you." I showed it, and she rang me up and continued, "And I'll likely never see you again."

"Oh, I can come in more often, no prob. Promise to ask for my ID every time, and it will be like this affirmation."

"This is my last day, buddy. I was here until we could get a new hire, and we got a new hire. She starts on Monday, and I'll be working my new job."

"Some competing booze place?"

"No, no, work that means something to me, work I can smile proudly about. I'll be doing rec-work at Alz-spice, like Alzheimer's meets Hospice, together at last."

A RESIDENT NAMED IRENE was more or less tricked into being here—so healthy and always stretching at seventy-two, but coming up with an enemies list all day and keeping tissue in her shoes, her son told her she was going to get her hair done, and now she lives with us. She will cut pictures from the newspaper and tabloids of men she thinks are me, all ages and ethnicities, curly-haired construction workers or sit-com daddies; they are often smiling with a woman by their side. I always take them in fun and tell her that I am collecting them for a scrapbook, and I will do this, I know, as she gets closer to the worst parts of the disease. When I get a picture, I take it home and show it to Jean, who laughs at the well-intended silliness and makes fun of me, or she did for the first ten clippings. The ones I bring home are now more erotic, with young dudes holding up bikini girlfriends or middle-aged lovers walking hand in hand along a bridge. Irene will write out WAY TO GO and LOOKS LIKE SHE LOVES YOU DON'T HURT HER all along the corners. It has become a little embarrassing, but I liked the attention that seemed to come from a scissored world. I tucked the most recent excised picture of me and the actress Julianne Moore into the book Jean was reviewing, in the first pages after the dust jacket, like some bookmark.

AT WORK, I SAW that liquor store girl walking around the floor, getting to know the residents, sitting with everyone at the lunch table. As I entered, my boss walked over to me and asked me to show her around, inform her on every duty, and let her shadow me for a few hours. The girl knew me right away, her eyes kind of narrowed in recognition, but she didn't know if we'd met in a class we shared or in a bar, and then I said, "Liquor store."

"Oh, wow, you work here. You didn't you tell me the other night."

"I wasn't totally sure you were talking about this place, and I don't like to talk any kind of shop unless I'm on the clock."

"Well, did you punch in yet?"

"Yep, so no excuses now. Let me walk you around and show you where we keep the ring toss."

Toni was a student of psychology, not currently enrolled because she'd just come back from a trip to Uruguay. The university she was attending had its points of specialty, geography and business. Lots of people said they were going to get their basics there and then move on, but that's not what Toni was saying. She was going to finish up her degree by the spring and then get her master's there and set up shop like Lucy in the Snoopy panels. She was going to work with kids; she loved all her nieces and wanted to be around the years before skepticism and arousal took hold.

In the daylight, she looked like she deserved these worlds. She was young but not so much a girl that she didn't also look like a woman with her time and money in order. She was pretty, with large eyes, dimples at her smile, black hair, and a straight nose that didn't go out or in and so looked to me like a job, but no one would get a job so straight. At the liquor store, she looked casually sinister, aloof, and then pained to be at any register. Here, she looked like she belonged to the world of comforting.

I took her into Irene's room to introduce her, and Irene started complimenting me on my beautiful wife. "Thanks, yeah, she is a knockout, but we're not even close. As the days go on, we may have less and less to do with one another." Toni looked at me, puzzled and slightly put-off, but still smiling. No one knew I was doing this other job, working with people like Denny. I had been here on time every day for over a year, but I believed with a terrific certainty that I would soon put in my two weeks.

JEAN WAS ON THE bed reading a Marguerite Duras collection of short essays on her drinking, her face, time spent in Hanoi, and *The Atlantic Man.*

Jean was in a languorous pose, her legs slightly bent at the knees, her head held up by her palm, elbow propped down on the untucked covers over the mattress. Jean was wearing nothing, but this was typical. In philosophy, Jean might as well have identified herself as a nudist, but it wasn't anything she ever thought too much about. I was very used to her naked body in all kinds of light and shade and, once in a while, I let myself appreciate her as if she were a girl I had only just discovered. I sat down by her and put my hand on her thigh. She kept reading. I kissed her shoulders, and she moved a little to straighten up. I knew that more kissing wasn't going to lead to anything; Jean was busy, and I was tired, and what I really wanted was to be on this side of the bed and think about her for a few minutes before I got up to see what we might eat together.

Denny and I were at the library. We were getting him signed up for a library card. He already knew how to do all these computer tricks, but I just wanted him to see the books and magazines, and then we walked on into the video sections. I pointed out shelf after shelf of outdated and obsolete expressions of media like slide projectors and laserdiscs. This section of the library was my favorite because it was as quiet as the rest of the place, but there was almost no one walking; it was like a museum. We used an old VCR on the level three side of Alz-spice, the house where the residents were really just sleeping and tapping the sides of the wall. I grabbed a few Marx Brothers flicks and walked Denny over to the check-out counter.

As always, when I got to that space, I felt as if that NO TALKING library rule was suddenly lifted. I asked Denny about the situation with that girl he liked. He'd started talking to her friends like I'd suggested, and now he talks to this one girl whose eyes look closed, whose dad runs a T-shirt business out of his garage, and whose mom teaches the guitar from the living room. School is this girl's only free space, and she won't even talk to her old friends now because she likes spilling her guts to Denny so much; it is just those two at the table. Denny didn't know if he liked the way this had turned out, but he was used to eating with her now, and the semester was almost over anyway.

We filled out his application for a library card. The lady at the desk, smiling like she thought he was my boy or nephew, gave Denny a temporary card; he checked out an illustrated *Aesop's Fables* and a Dick Tracy coffee-table book, and we drove off.

In my car, there were a dozen individually cut-out pictures of women Irene thought I was married to or having flings with. There was some guy on the beach with Drew Barrymore and another guy wrestling with his dog, and the words, all written bluntly for me: HAPPY MAN WHAT'S YOUR SECRET and SHE KNOWS SHE HAS YOU NOW. Denny had them in his fingers, holding them up to the orange dusk light outside, and said, "These would be good laminated. Do you think you could ever part with them?"

"I was planning on sticking all this month's car trash in a notebook, but sell me on your idea, man."

"There are lots of bits of paper everywhere, but you get them with that plastic, and they become something else. I want to get them, and if I start on a book, but get tired, I want to know how far I got if I gave up, or how far to go if I like what I am reading."

"Bookmarks," I said.

"I know about bookmarks. This is something else, like book bibs."

I dropped Denny off, walking up to the door with him to say hello to his mother who was smiling that grateful smile. It was just her and Denny, and it was hard to go off to work and difficult to make it work with a kid like Denny; you could love him to death, but you'd have to always be watching and figuring him out because your kid is going to stare at this microwave all day and then decide to look up recipes online, and you have to be working. Mom smiled at me, so happy that her boy was back and so happy that she had that six-hour break. I knew we were the same age, methods of choice, and birth control putting us in different worlds.

"I'll see you next Saturday," I said and drove off, knowing I would pass the liquor store and not go in; there was no reason to go in. If I went in, I would just spend money, and I had drinks at home, and Jean was home, but I would coast by to see who was working the register now.

Curfew

The Christmas lights were still plugged in and going at Mike's home. In this town, a touristy spot betwixt two major cities with a water park, a Sights and Sounds of Christmas parade, Oktoberfest, and an outlet mall that gets neon scary for each season, we tend to keep the lights going for a good while longer than is acceptable in gratitude and commercial applause for the sudden swell of the economy. It was typical of my neighbors to have the lights going past Three Kings' Day, but they all came down that last week of January. It was now February, and I was thinking about what I was going to get Sonia for Valentine's day. The last three years had been me trying to bake her a cake, and I have no taste for how cake should come out, so the resulting pastry-like pie is a messy joke about inappropriate sugar usage. I was thinking about the cakes when I noticed the lights came on at Mike's. It was 9 p.m., which meant it was dark outside, and I was just staring at his home from my window like a guy looking for a secret go-ahead sign, when a glitter of popcorn-colored lights went up around his mailbox and door, with a few lights in the grass, the chain of glow interrupted by some that had gone dead.

Looking at the grass and the unraked winter leaves, I suddenly felt the quick worry that some tragedy had befallen Mike sometime between holidays and, unless he had some very quiet company, he had been alone in the house all this time.

Sonia was out with a couple of college girlfriends. Sometimes I'd join them for a walk around the high school track near our house, the same track where Sonia's cousin Gina used to win prizes doing relays and jumping hurdles. Now, she joins their group for their Wednesday night walking routine, or they all go out for dinner at this Germanic-themed café called Rommel's that keeps votive candles on the tables, serves black bread with black beer, and plays Kurt Weill kink and *The Genius of Jankowski*. Honestly, I could offer no valuable anecdote or gossip to further their fun, so most nights, I'd stay in.

Still staring out my window into Mike's home, I noticed the play of insect light, blue-white, blue-white-red, behind a dark window glass. Oh, this guy wasn't in any trouble; he was watching TV.

I could call him up, but I didn't know Mike's number. Sonia had it on her cell, and I never knew it at all. She'd given him a ride to see his daughter on one of his visiting days. Later, he called the house to thank me for letting her do it like I was in some kind of control of her and divulged, "I have these times when I can see Dawn like at a hospital or museum tour of some traveling Van Gogh lithographs. And I can't talk so free like I'm talking here when I am up close to her. I act guarded and say fake-sounding stuff to my kid. She's just turned nine. Get enough sleep, I say. Try and read a book a week. I never read *any* books when I was nine, and my smart kid knows it."

Mike was an emotionally distraught man, a divorced father with limited visitation rights and a car that sometimes wouldn't run, and here I had neglected to even say Happy New Year, because—where *was* Mike in this new year?

I thought I saw the light behind his window go black, and then I was out the door, outside my house, walking in steady strides like I was about to commence an evening's constitutional. Now my fingers where touching the lights around his mailbox, wanting to nonviolently tug them out of their socket, but I thought, irrationally, maybe these lights were all that were keeping Mike alive. I rang his doorbell, ready to feel for unlocked windows if there was no answer, but someone appeared at the door.

A woman with shoulder-length red hair and large, somber, not unlovely eyes, she looked to be in her mid-twenties, and she looked tired.

She looked as if someone was coming to relieve her of a terrible duty. She greeted me with a hello that sounded like a hip variation of "halo" and "hollow" but in my head just registered as "high/low."

"Is Mike here?" I asked, and felt ten years old.

There is a kind of smile that is no smile at all, but a pursed mouth of cloaked indictment, a smile as incredulous as it seems honest; this girl at Mike's place was good at smiling this way and perhaps could smile no other way.

"Mike's not home." She narrowed her large hazel eyes into what I took as joke accusation and added, "You didn't know?"

I couldn't gauge the level of put-on, but I didn't mind the feeling, like an electrical charge coming from the space between this lady and me.

"I don't know my neighbors that well."

She turned, tilted her head out to see who or what might be behind me. "Well, Mike knows you pretty well. That house, right?" She pointed at my home. "You and your wife give him rides sometimes. He told me that I should let either one of you in if you come by. So," and she gestured with her left palm for me to enter. I hadn't ever been in this house. Of course, I had been invited dozens of times. I don't know what the inside of any of my neighbors' homes looked like. "Mike's not home, and my name's Kate. You want a drink while I fill you in?"

I said, "No, that's okay," but as soon as this girl started her story, I had to interrupt and suggest that maybe I'd better take one of whatever she was having.

While she poured rum into a glass of dark soda and ice for me, Kate spoke. "The guy was always quiet around me; for a long time I thought he was being a snob or like he didn't care to meet me 'cause I'm this new person that he's not going to be friends with anyhow. Then, about a month after we started working together, he comes around, and we get to know each other because we keep rubbing elbows at the soda machine, and there is an attraction that makes that awkward; it turns out we both like funny movies and sad music, we both studied accounting before switching majors and dropping out, we have mutual friends in the pool business, and this girl by my desk tells me that really it's that he likes me *a lot*, but that he feels embarrassed for liking me. He's been divorced for two years now and, having such problems with his ex, he never gets to see his kid; getting with anyone new would make that worse. I like him too, but I am living with someone. I don't get along with kids, and I don't want any drama, but it has become clear that to acknowledge the crush is a high for us both. So we have lunch right outside the office one day, sitting on the steps, and talk out the tangles and decide to be like that kind of star-crossed friend to one another, fated to never be more but respecting each other's appeal. It made working in the billing department fun."

The girl had a set of photos in a black shoebox set by the couch next to a pair of midnight blue slippers; when she opened the lid, the smell of peppermint emanated as if she kept scented candles and specialty tea in with the pictures. "There: Mike and me and Mike himself. I took them all at work. See how good he looks in this shot, up against the copy machine like he fucking owns the place? We were never going to be together, but we made each other happy, how we talked each other up to others and fed each other lines in private. When he'd walk by me, I'd sometimes touch his shoulder, and he would always tell me I looked like that actress who always goes to award shows with her brother. There were many compliments. I loved going to work. I felt like we were getting away with something really great and private."

I examined the photos. Mike was smiling, shy, and genuine. He looked happy. Every time I saw him watering the lawn or going out for the mail, he looked like he was trying to memorize dialogue for a play he was thrown into. "You two should have just been together."

The girl drank from her own glass, nodding in a way that seemed opposed to any idea she was actually entertaining. "You know, I think I wanted that at some point, to see what we could be together. And he did, too, along the way, but never at the same time. Also, we were no good at relationships. I was still in one that wasn't working, and he had sworn them off completely. It was a good time knowing he was there and that I was there, a heaven time to count on each other's presence." Kate began to shuffle-stack the photographs together like she was playing cards and placed them back in the shoebox she had on her lap.

"Things got worse for us both. His ex, Sharon, said she got a new job and was going to move out of the city, out of the state, and then kept giving him lots of possible locations like a crazy trick to mix him up. He knew eventually he'd know where they were going to move because of the child support checks, but he was getting nervous, and he knew he wasn't going to be able to see his girl anymore.

"My boyfriend, Joseph, was pressuring me to get married. We'd been living together for three years. I didn't want to and tried to avoid the talk all the time, but that was impossible. It got bad. What was always just smooth speculation about our future became threats, dark ultimatums, and then he just split, left a lot of his junk and left me with the rent. Joseph moved out the same week that Mike's wife took off with his kid. Mike and I were now alone—problem-free, in a sense, at least I felt that way—but still besought with the penalties of all this dread. Mike was so quiet now at work, so still at his desk and shocked-looking, like he'd lost something forever. It was as if we'd never been interested in each other at all.

"I was in a fixed fear that Joseph would come back to the house at any time, middle of the night, Christmas Eve, whenever. I never thought he was going be violent or anything, but with him gone, I realized what a joke the last couple of years had been. I really felt that I didn't need him, didn't enjoy him, and I didn't want him to come back and try to talk things out. I knew that was going to happen because after a week, he called, and even though I never answered the phone, he kept calling, leaving soft and pleading messages. Mike and I thought we should go out now, for real, and talk about what we were. We could go to a bar or a park and get to know each other in ways that we couldn't before, so we did. We went out three times, but it wasn't happening. Outside of work, *we* didn't work. We would talk on the phone as we watched the same movie, just like that scene in *When Harry Met Sally*, but for us, it was a way we were coming apart.

"That same coworker who told me Mike liked me asked if we had been secretly dating and had a bad secret breakup. I said no, that wasn't true, but I felt that she had somehow gotten to the truth of something.

"One evening, after a day in which we'd spoken not two words to one another, we drove off from work, and both of us had the same idea to drop in on each other at home. I came over here, and he went over to my place. He left his door open because he always does that, so I walked in, looked at his place, and noticed all the vacation spot postcards on the fridge, the Escher prints he decorated his walls with, the Stephen King paperbacks on the glass coffee table. Was I prepared to get to know the most mundane parts of this guy's life? I sat on this couch and, waiting for him to return, fell asleep, so comfortable; just before drifting off, I felt like he loved me. That was the first time I ever felt that around him. I never did.

"I woke fifteen minutes later because he was calling me; Mike was at my house, outside my place. I never leave the door open, so he was outside. He'd wanted to see me and talk about what we were, which he deemed a very shallow kind of friendship. He told me that his wife had left a message on his cell and then hadn't answered it because the number was unidentified. 'She knows I don't pick up on any call that says restricted,' he said. She left him a P.O. box address and said that Dawn was fine and that she would be in touch soon with further info. I told him a way he could crawl over the fence and get into my place from a kitchen window. 'You can wait there for me. I'm at Kohl's department store,' I lied to him. 'I will be there after I return this dress I bought last week that looks bad on me.'"

The girl held up a picture of herself in which she was wearing a blue dress that looked loose and comfy, the one she was pretending to return, I guessed, and shook my head. She met him like she said, and they discussed her fears that this old boyfriend of hers would show up, and they talked about the way their friendship had effectively ended, leaving them with the feelling of ruined romance without the pain.

"We sat on my couch, and Mike held his head in his hands and looked at his feet. 'But we know things about each other, Mike,' I said. 'We know things we shouldn't have to tell new people, information I would never want to explain to a new person. I never want to see Joseph again, not even for that last goodbye. Can you stay at my place for a while?' I asked. 'You don't have to do anything, just be there for him when he comes to the door or answer the phone if he calls. And he *will* call; he's been calling all week. I don't want to have to do that. I should not have to do that.' I thought Mike was smiling hard at this proposal until I realized he was crying.

"I let him go through it, then let him speak. 'I used to call Dawn every other night at 9 p.m. to see if she was getting ready for bed. I'd ask her about her day and tell her sweet dreams, goodnight, baby. We would talk better on the phone. I don't know why. Maybe *I'm* just better on the phone, like how I'm on the phone at work. It's like how we can talk on the phone, but here in your place, I'm not even looking you in the eye. I keep trying to call back the number, but it keeps going to voicemail, and Sharon hasn't even set up her inbox, so I don't know if it's even her phone. This guy, Joseph, he just wants to know that he can see you sometime,' Mike said, 'that you are still in the world. He just wants to know that if he walks up to your house, you are there. He wanted to marry you, Kate. That's how close he got. He just hurts.'

"I felt a bravery come over me that I knew would vanish in two seconds and said, '*You* can talk to him if he comes by. You can let him talk to you about me.' Mike stared at a ceramic Snoopy, this prize I'd kept since I was six. I can't throw it out because the brother I don't speak to anymore won it for me at a church fair, and anytime I put it out for a garage sale, no one ever buys it. 'Until Joseph comes by, and you talk to him, you should live here a while, get it through to him that I am gone. I will go by your house and make sure someone's always home, in case your ex-wife shows or calls to tell you anything about your daughter.'"

I drank the last of my drink, and Kate got up to get me a refill, but I shook my head.

"So now it has been a while, months. My ex calls a lot, and Mike and Joseph have gotten to know each other; they talk often. They get through things on the phone. Joseph has no plans to try to see me and doesn't ask Mike where I am anymore. He keeps saying he's going over to pick up a fish tank and a pair of binoculars that he left, but then he doesn't, like he's putting something off. They need each other, I think, in a way that I never needed either of them."

I looked around Mike's place; what had looked clean and organized on first entrance now looked absolutely frozen in time. "There is a room back there where I keep a few things, some clothes and a laptop. The rest of the place I have not touched because, when Joseph gets his stuff, Mike's coming right back here. I don't want him to ever feel that this place isn't his. I sleep here on this couch every night. I turn the Christmas lights on when I am about to turn in. It's a sign for Mike if he drives by, so he doesn't wake me if he wants to come in. I asked about the neighbors when it seemed like I was going to be here indefinitely, and Mike said he didn't know anyone, but if anyone did come by to see what was up, it would be you or your wife, and I should tell either one of you what has happened to him and who I am."

I got up to leave, and Kate saw me to the door. I saw that Sonia was not yet home. I prepared myself for a description of our new neighbor and, before leaving, asked if Mike's ex-wife had ever called or come by. Kate said no, never.

"Someone calls around this time every other night, doesn't say anything, and then hangs up. But I know it isn't her."

The Offices of Fang and Claw

Those of us who thought we knew Harold fancied ourselves privy to some deep fount of lucky information. We alone, the three of us that ever spoke to him during those first weeks when he came back to our world, felt as if we were the grand recipients of some hermit's reversal.

At twenty-five, he had more-or-less taken a vow of silence, having given up on the idea of being an actor or singer. Having also come to realize that he never cared enough about the physical preservation of his watercolor works to see that they went undamaged if they went unsold, Harold decided he wanted to write.

Julia, whom he would later marry and make very happy but back then was simply dating and making very sad, was delighted by the news. She always thought Harold, whether in a studio or on a stage, was wasting his talent for showing off in the wrong medium. "It's that you want people to admire you as a thinker, and you haven't thought anything out. I'd love it if you wrote. I'd love to tell people that you wrote. What do you want to write?"

"My memoirs," Harold said, not joking, which of course made Julia laugh. She'd regret laughing at the last words he would ever speak to her,—that is, until he gave up on the project of scribbling in silence and decided to come back to the friends he'd abandoned—the last *spontaneous* words he would speak to her, at any rate.

Harold had the last words with each of us that week. I met him at the gallery across from a newsstand I was hoping would hire me after I graduated (the newsstand, not the gallery; I had no illusions about what doors might open up for me and my Communications degree). We stood before a forest green and pearl-hued collage of oils on cardboard. "This stinks," he said, and I nodded. "No, man, this *really* stinks, like turpentine and old sandwich wrappers. I can't look at this anymore. Not if I have to smell it, too."

I suggested we go for a walk, get a coffee and then a beer, and then visit with Anne, a girl I was in love with, because—and I know this is sort of impossible sounding and probably has much more to do with my perception rather than her reality—Anne reminded me of several sitcom women I had crushes on as a child while watching TV Land reruns alone on those Saturday nights my parents wanted to go on dates. I presumed back then that they were going on dates with each other, but now, as I have breakfast with Dad every Sunday in his apartment and then dinner with Mom at the old house, I know much better. Anne could sometimes resemble Samantha from that *Bewitched* show, but that last week when we were speaking to Harold, she was starting to look to me a lot like that mother from *The Partridge Family*. Anne was someone who cared nothing about me but was someone I decided upon first meeting that I wanted to be around as much as possible, regardless of any reciprocal affection. These were the years when I could firmly say that I adored Anne; later, displaced from my devotion, I would, of course, look back at her and wonder about the infatuation, but back then, I was content with my longing. Fixating on just one real woman who reminded me of numerous fake women was a way of control; I knew that Anne knew that about me too, and she did not make fun of me for this fault.

"If I see Anne, I will be forced to explain to her how I have given up on acting, singing, and painting and have now settled into my role as a writer," explained Harold.

I laughed, too, just like Julia had laughed. We would all of us wonder about how our reactions to his news might have changed everything for him, for us, but in the end, we came to realize we had no control over Harold's fate, and that it had always been some kind of self-flattery to pretend we ever did.

Harold didn't say anything back when we laughed but kind of nodded like he was expecting the response.

"So you quit painting because it cost too much and everything has already been done, and you quit singing because you could never really sing and have so far been lucky enough that no one caught on, but why have you decided to give up acting?" I asked him, sensing I'd offended the man.

Harold brought me over with a curled index finger to show me a section of his scalp over which he then started to slowly tap. "There are several white hairs now. They weren't here last year. This whole act that I could *ever* act was based on appearances I cannot keep up."

I never knew Harold was as vain as all this and told him as much.

The next time I saw him, I realized how true this might have been. Harold was disheveled and looked ready to offend. He was writing, always writing in spiral notebooks. He worked in a warehouse when he wasn't writing. He moved boxes and didn't speak to anyone. He ate out often. He drank alone in an apartment. We learned about this phase of his life only after the fact, when he'd completed his memoirs and decided to make contact with us.

We met at Julia's house. It had been seven years, and she was recently divorced from the editor of a home décor magazine she'd interned under shortly after Harold disappeared. I showed up with Anne, with whom I was still happily in love, and who had come around over the years to finding me important enough to phone almost every evening, to talk out the kinks in her afternoon comp classes, and listen to me talk about the pressures of hiring on reliable summer help for the newsstand I now owned.

Harold formally announced that he was done with writing and was now ready to, if we would have him, be a friend to us again, to be the kind of man who could enjoy people, food, affairs, and the feel of a book in his hands. Julia took his face in her hands, kissed him in front of Anne and me, and then walked him outside so they could be alone.

If Harold looked as good or better than he had ever looked (and really, he looked relaxed), Julia was very aware that she had slackened in her appearance and confessed to Anne—who told me everything anyway—that she wanted to be the girl she was when she had first become fascinated with interior design and started to study photography, to ebb over whoever she had become these last years. This desire manifested itself in a manic ritual. Julia would spread old photographs of herself along her bed, deciding what her truest images were at every state: as a toddler, as a preteen, when she first met Harold, and she'd keep these pictures by a set of magazine cut-outs of women like Phoebe Cates and Asia Argento, women she had been told over the years she resembled. Julia would drink when she did this and sometimes even listen to music.

The two were inseparable for a week, and Julia was trying, as best she could, to keep up with the new contentment Harold carried. She went on walks with him, started to diet, quit smoking, and proposed that they move in together. Very shortly after all this, they decided to marry and, in fact, eloped; when Anne and I were rightfully offended not to have been invited to the wedding, Julia confessed drunkenly on the phone to Anne, who later relayed it to me, that these days, she was uncomfortable being seen by anyone who knew her longer than a few weeks, and the idea of having to look the way a bride is supposed to look made her panic.

Soon after the wedding, Harold started to work in a local law firm doing paralegal chores and had decided to go back to school to become the lawyer he claimed he always should have been. Even though he'd never expressed any interest in law before, no one in our clique was surprised by this announcement.

Anne and I went to see Harold and Julia one last time before never seeing them again. At that dinner, I sat with Anne at the end of the table and listened to Harold talk about his new happiness while he held up a glass of sparkling water as if to privately toast himself. I felt a feeling perhaps hadn't ever felt come over me: Jealousy.

Two nights later, Anne called me up and said we needed to talk about Harold in person, not on the phone. She came over and said, "First, you need to explain why you insist on being, as you say, in love with me."

I went through the old story. Being in love with someone you had no chance with was very motivating. It could almost be a life's work. "The love I have for you has kept me happy for nearly a decade, and I wouldn't trade that time for anything," I explained.

Anne looked at me like she wanted to cry and nodded. "Make love to me."

"Why?"

"So you can get over me."

"Never."

Anne shook her head and walked over to the couch and unbuttoned her blouse and pulled a spiral notebook, the color of green jello, out of her purse.

"What do you have there?" I asked, trying to talk my way out of arousal.

"This is from Harold's memoirs. This is part sixteen of an eighty-nine-series set. Julia found it this morning, read some of it, and asked me to take a look."

"I'm not reading my best friend's diary," I said, realizing as I spoke that I could no longer claim Harold as even a casual acquaintance and that I knew next to nothing about him.

"You don't get it. This isn't anything like a diary, or a confession, or anything close to a memoir. These spiral notebooks are numbered and even dated, but all Harold has ever written about are events that haven't happened. This one is for October of next year."

Anne rolled her head back and forth, licked her lips, and read: "*"I came home to find my wife talking to Lisa; it was clear that they were discussing how they would make this work—make the* three *of us. It was a situation I wanted to end, a situation I would end, regardless of the feelings of everyone involved, mine, theirs..."*"

Anne looked at me; a tress of her damp hair dangled over her left eye and lay tucked behind her ear.

"You know who Lisa is?"

I shook my head.

"Julia says the girl who answers the phone when she calls for Harold is named Lisa, or Eliza...she's not sure. But *you're* in here. Wanna see?"

I didn't and said as much.

Anne shook her head. "Yeah, okay," she said, turned some pages, stretched, and sat up. "This is the part that *really* scared Julia, some business about how she has a favorite morning show and eats candy in bed. Check this out: *'increasingly, I worried that if she didn't watch it she would become a diabetic like her sister who hadn't updated her Facebook image in three years.'*

"Wow, that freaked her out more than the *ménage à trois* thing?" I asked, hoping Anne would put the notebook down and switch topics to paper grading.

Anne shook her head, flipped through some pages, and read on: "*After she was denied tenure, the blonde professor took to swimming, and to coloring her hair. In the relay pool, she would hold her breath and gnash her teeth as if bobbing for apples, and told herself that she dyed her hair because all the swimming was turning her silken locks a sulky shade,. But when she was honest with herself, she knew that she had, in fact, always associated brunettes with brains and bravado, and maybe—she feared and hated herself for fearing—other people did as well.*' Guess who that was about?"

I didn't have to guess, and we both swore to never forgive the man who in his years of isolation amid warehouse work had taken creative pains to forge our fates with runny ink along college-ruled pages.

Anne and I made love. "It's all about the future," Anne said as we pulled apart, "and it's all about fear." We were quiet then. We hugged each other on the couch and continued to kiss in lonely ways for several hours before falling asleep.

As I tasted the chlorine from the pool on her skin and understood how alone I was going to feel from now on, I noticed for the first time in the near-decade I'd been infatuated with Anne that she looked quite a bit like Barbara Eden from that *I Dream of Jeannie* show, only now with dark brown hair.

Red Lines Drawn in the Blue Room

Today around 4:30 a.m., I gathered together all the obituaries I had written over the last three years, which, when I poured them out of their shoe box shell, tallied up to forty-seven. I was looking for frequently used, overused words of mourning, words like *august* and *magnanimous* and variants on a phrase like *a boon to the community*. It was no secret that there was a formula for making these obits sing: be understated and don't blurt out that the dead guy *went to Jesus* or *joined his loved ones in his new home in heaven*, even if the dead guy might have really wanted his obit writer to let this information be known, and even if this sentiment was his last goddamned wish. What the hell does this dead guy know now that he is no more, and what does he have to say about *anything* now that he is gone and at the mercy of my laptop? Understatement is the sole undertaking, and it is far more delicate a project than the work executed by the actual undertaker.

The word *cosmopolitan* appeared three times in my three years of obit work to describe three people that I knew for a fact had never left the county, let alone the country. A wedding planner named Wilma was *savvy*, but so, too, was a carpenter named Pete.

Had all this understated overestimation been underhanded? What crimes had I committed by dancing up the dead?

I wasn't up all night thinking it over. I had fallen asleep at 8 p.m. and slept until 4 a.m. I lay in bed, telling myself that I should lie prone and sleep more and more, but I finally started to get hungry. I had not been hungry in a week, not since my Aunt Teresa died, and I was once again asked to write a little something for the church paper. This meant I was also going to write a little something for the actual paper, the one that used to get tossed house to house for free on Wednesdays but now can only be read online. I felt that being this awake was a sign of health that I should not brush off. I should make coffee, make water, and then look at three years of my obits.

When Aunt Teresa, who had been living in my place for the last six months, died, the insurance UPS-ed over a cardboard box of frozen TV dinners to my front door: blueberry and grain bars, frozen bags of what I took to be powdered milk, and microwavable peas and carrots and meatloaf plastic hospital food trays that I will offer to Meals on Wheels. The package arrived at 6 p.m. on the day of her burial, three hours after my aunt was in the ground. The church sisters were unloading the flowers for her service into my living room to keep them in an air-conditioned space because the church turns off its A/C at night to save on the electric bill. I was planning on letting Victoria Temple keep the flowers after the service, but I was only going to be able to do that by bringing all the flowers back to the church on Sunday, just like I brought them in for the memorial service. It would be the same toxic-plant, sticky spray in my face as I hauled roses and fronds in the 104 degree South Texas heat, the same vase water spilling on my nutmeg-hued Sansabelt polyester church pants. Then came all the hand shaking and me trying to wash my hands so hard in the bathroom where the church never allows hot water. Only the cold pours out. I used to think they were afraid of getting sued for the potential burn on parishioners. Now, I think that the church is just against anything hot: hot blood, hot sauce, all the church clothes are so hot, and hell is so hot, and the coffee you have to wait wait wait for to cool before you drink.

The instant coffee the insurance shipped my way was the first good consciously hot thing I had tempered in a week. I boiled a pan of water and clipped a cube of that frozen milk into a ceramic cup that said #1 SON and stirred its bark-brown dehydrated flecks into a swirl with my index finger before poring over the pile of obits.

The words I wrote for the dead were never changed in the actual paper. Words like *steadfast* and phrases like *years of observance* stayed put. In the church paper, someone always took a Vis-a-Vis marker to the print of the page I submitted and changed up a lot of nouns and verbs into insulating coffin cush. Now *Jim Maricone died at home* goes: *Jim Maricone joined his Lord*; now *Tobe Thurgood succumbed to his illness* becomes *Coach Thurgood separated from his earthly ties*, and Gertrude Sullivan no longer even got to pass away but had to *graduate to her new home*. Look, I am no atheist, and I find nothing duller than a sarcastic and skeptical man proclaiming his doubt before a crowd that could not care less and always expects more. Repeat and rephrase: nothing is more offensive to me than an un-funny fellow cheapshot-ing his way to cheap laughs by poking holes where there never was a solid. Bill Maher, George Carlin. Haha, fuck you. It is no feat to defeat the faithful, but before being a man of God, I am still just a man, and I really don't like it when my words are changed.

The obit I put together for Aunt Teresa was composed of three lines that told the world that she was 68-years old, that she was an elementary school teacher and a lifelong member of the Iglesia Apostólica, and that she was preceded in death by her father Gregario, her mother Susanna, and her sister Flora I know she has a brother named Mateo who lives upstate, but they never spoke, so I wrote that Teresa was survived by me.

The bargain I made with Victoria Temple was that if I wrote obits for the church, if I was their newsletter guy for the dead, for a pamphlet we called *Holy Ghost Post*, I would not be expected to actually attend the services and the ceremonies. For three years, this was how I managed. *So much death, right? And I have to really see into their souls to write out their charms and habits. You can understand how it messes me up to be so involved and then have to be in church too. So, please don't expect me to show up on any grieving Sunday.*

It worked until Teresa died. Teresa, not my only aunt but the only one I kept talking to, the one who drove me around when my license was suspended and I still had to get to work. After her baby sister died —her sister, my mother—I thought I should look in on her all the time because, even though she had that brother in El Paso and a cousin very close in Pharr, she had no one else.

Her stroke and her slow dissolve and how quickly it made sense for me to invite her into my mother's old room made me know full well that it was I who had no one else. The last six months were me helping her to the door so she could try to get the mail and the paper and heating up *caldo* for her. I called the girl who would bathe her and help her to the car that took her to church, which was near enough to walk to, and then would meet her at the curb when she was being dropped back off from service. We would watch a mega-church prosperity preacher named Calvin Cochise talk about tithing, and then we would watch a PBS cooking show she liked that was all about Italian bread. She would go to sleep at 9 p.m., and I would flip around talk shows until I found an Adult Swim cartoon I liked and drink vodka tonics alone and sleep five hours, then get up when I heard her moving around in the morning.

I was expected to be a pallbearer at her funeral, say some kind words about this kind woman, help with the metal fold-out chairs for the coffee klatch memorial and, of course, write the obit.

The congregation at Victoria Temple is small. When I used to go every Sunday, I would count heads, and I would always count around twenty-eight people: three families for sure, no children unless it was Easter or Christmas or some young, out-of-wedlock woman had just given birth and was staying with a family that attended, and this woman had no problem wearing a *velo* and listening to Latino glossolalia. It is a dying church, but everyone knows someone who is dying and, regardless of the attendance or church membership, if you are a visitor and bring that doomed name up to Pastor Laffy, he will pray for the dying. He will do a deathbed visit and secure perhaps as much as $500 for any funeral service. The one catch, and it catches no one but me, is that we will have an obit in our newsletter.

The Verger——the alternative weekly that ceased print and went online after an editorial schism over a food column and some in-house havoc regarding rogue ad men who managed to sabotaged the paper's ADMIN—has no problem publishing the obits the way I write them. I send all death notices in as if they were letters-to-the-editor, and the obits are in need of zero edits. I include a picture of the dead and send everything in anonymously like some vigilante on a digital vigil, and the words go up. No problem. Maybe three or four people recall the dead and leave a line of *bless you, now* and *forevermore, we will hold you in our thoughts and prayers*, but sometimes there are so many people that want to leave their feeling of loss, it blows my mind. How could anyone with fifty-seven R.I.P.s have ever just died of pneumonia? But it happens and will happen again. This morning, looking over the forty-seven obits I have kept in a shoe box and will soon move into the scrapbook my Aunt Teresa once intended to keep recipes, I know that I will no longer have a part in any of it.

I was supposed to make an appointment to speak directly with Laffy, the pastor of Victoria Temple, but saw I his powder-blue Oldsmobile outside the church parking lot this morning. The light was on in the office; it was 5:40 a.m., so the man had slept over. There was a room that was supposed to be a sanctuary for illegals okay with cleaning up around the pews for room and board and for anyone running from the cops who needed to get their story straight before the big turn-in, which would, of course, be encouraged. I often dreamed of this room, which I only saw two times.

Once, a woman from another church from another city in the same denomination was in hiding from an abusive guy—or that was the story that we all heard on Sunday. I heard the story, even though I wasn't in service, from my aunt and others. I actually saw the girl in the room when I was coming in to turn in that week's obit, and maybe the girl in the blue room was in hiding, or maybe she was coming down, or maybe she was just Laffy's guest. The room was cobalt-chalk azure with its own always-blowing window air-conditioner even though the whole building was climate controlled. There was an ochre-stained wood twin bed, a walnut-brown plastic mini-fridge, a white trash bag of folded towels, jeans, and t-shirts, and a calendar, always a new calendar. Last year's was the images of Jerusalem; this year it was bluebonnets of Texas. Pastor Laffy slept there on the nights in between service, especially since his wife left to do mission work in Argentina.

The other time I saw the blue room, I was walking through to drop off an obit and saw Laffy asleep on the floor, not even on the bed but conked out atop a crayon-blue-colored exercise mat like he was doing yoga and had passed out while attempting the corpse position. I placed the obit on the bed and decided to email my death notices to him from then on.

It is a testimony to Laffy's faith in God and man that he never locked the church doors. If you knew the right door to try, you could always get in.

It was not the front door. The front door had glass starting to crack when some Vacation Bible School brat tossed a rock at his sister and hit the church door instead. We used clear tape to hold the glass together. Later, a palsy-afflicted parishioner slammed the door hard because this guy could only get anywhere by slamming hard and walking hard, plugging choice into every step, so we needed to reach into the donation can for new-glass-door money. That one door stays locked now, for sure. The doors behind the church, the doors by the air-conditioner near the green recycle can that is never taken to the street, and that one backdoor are open all the time.

I walked in and looked at my cell phone to see the time: 6:00 a.m. Laffy would want someone to wake him if he wasn't already up.

I lightly knocked on the office sanctuary door, started to knock again, and the door opened up. Pastor Laffy was serious, squinting for sight, and then smiled quickly once he recognized me.

"Brother Bert, I didn't know anyone would be meeting me this day for prayer or a prayer breakfast. I am woefully unprepared for prayer this day, but let us eat. Without a soul before me, I drink coffee and pace and wait for someone to join me for lunch, but you are here, so let us to the kitchen."

"Coffee is all I have time for," I said, having come prepared with a pocket of insurance-provided cereal bars.

Laffy shook his head, put his hand on my shoulder, and started to walk me down the hall as if there was something he did not want me to see in the cobalt chalk-white room.

I let him lead me to the kitchen where there was a radio on, a small radio with a cassette player and a Garbage Pail Kids sticker over its dial; the ugly cartoon had been rubbed off, but the puffy, parodic print of the red words *Gar age ids* was discernible. I felt ashamed that I used to buy those horrible stickers all the time. The radio was tuned very low to a static channel where I could hear a man talking in Spanish, slowly as if he were delivering a farmer's report in a silo. Laffy messed with the dial until I heard an "Alleluia!" and then some clapping and an organ; Laffy turned the knob down for the click off.

The pastor pushed a Styrofoam cup of coffee my way and bit open a tiny silver individual packet tube of Philadelphia Cream Cheese and squeezed the rich dairy over a sliced and already toasted bagel. Holding one half of his breakfast before his open mouth, he motioned down to the other half with his index finger to send me registry of his offering. He was waiting for me to allow him to eat.

I shook my head, sipped at my coffee, and watched Laffy chew.

On my walk over, I kept in mind that I only wanted to thank him for all he had done for my aunt's service, for all the rides he managed to get her for the church, and to tell him that now that she was gone, I would be cutting out. An *I appreciate it all, but this is my exit*, but instead of that style of straightforward, I started to lie. "Pastor, I will be leaving town very soon. I will be gone for months and months, and I cannot in good faith keep up with the obits."

Laffy kept chewing.

I went on. "I don't know how to go on with this work and not perhaps be in jeopardy of writing the wrong thing as I will be on the road and visiting so many people I have not seen in so long and—"

"Where will you be worshipping?" Pastor Laffy asked me. He didn't ask where I was going or tell me that he knew I was lying. He just asked me where I would put my prayers.

I didn't have the strength to say what I had planned on saying to him if he bugged me, which would have been something close to a Dr. Seuss kiss-off. *Anywhere but here, man, on a bench, on a boat, with a goat, in the pockets of my coat.* I just shrugged my shoulders and wondered aloud how many people were attending Victoria Temple these days. "So, how many are we now? I haven't been in a while. Are we still at twenty-eight?"

"Attendance was at forty-three last week, Bert, but I don't suppose you would know what goes on in this building."

"Hey, man, that was our deal," I said.

Laffy put a paper napkin to his lips and cleared his throat. "Attendance is up, Bert. I don't have to tell you that a lot of the brisk walk-in is because of the work you do for us and what you write about the departed. People read obits, and they read where the obits originate, even though you keep all that information out of the local rag like you're ashamed or in hiding. The obits you write get forwarded, get sent, and people see the name of our church. Maybe they send a thank you note, maybe they even stop by to say thanks in the flesh, and I show them that tape of what we were once when we were 200 strong. I tell them why we have stayed here on this land even after the split in '89, why Victoria Temple is a *living* church, and three out of every thirty-three that ponder the place are pilgrims. That's God, Bert, but that is also because of you."

I stared at the coffee pot that was still on and making a hissing sound even though there was no more coffee in it.

"Can I show you something, Bert?"

"Only if it is on my way out."

Pastor Lafcadio Gomez started to walk me to the blue sanctuary room where he had spent this night and who knows how many other nights, maybe sleeping, maybe not, but in utter accessibility to his flock and to anyone else who knew that the back door was always open. The blue room smelled of sweet-musk cologne samples and even smelled of the slick fashion magazines that would house them. Instinctively, I sat on the bed, which was made and tucked in a bounce-a-quarter, tight way because I was suddenly so tired, even though I had slept eight dreamless hours.

He opened a drawer and pulled out a slim phone book which covered the three towns that together fused a populous of 55,000 around Victoria Temple. Pastor Laffy placed the phone book to my left side and waited for me to pick it up to thumb through the pages. I noticed blue marker asterisk marks by certain names, then green marks, and then a few red slashes through some of the names that were also dotted with a green marker point.

I was on "Alvarez, Josie" when I realized that the blue marks were names of people who regularly attended Victoria Temple. I reasoned that the green dots were for people who visited, and then I knew that the red lines were for those who would not be back—whether that was by choice or not, these guys were stricken from the white pages of this phone book. I even knew one of the names of one of the red-line guys: Gabriel Soto. He was a kid I knew who used to hang out with me and my cousin, Sammy, over at Teresa's when we were nine, and she would bring us to Vacation Bible School in early August. I convinced him to come to church with me because I wanted a friend to go with me, and I got him to come by Victoria Temple because, in the summer, the building was cool; there were snacks, and there were girls and Bible-quote prizes.

Gabriel and I stopped talking in our twenties. Outside of the cage of adolescence, we had nothing in common. He got married at twenty-three when I was deciding how long I could hang around on campus before it would start to look ridiculous. At some point, Gabriel returned to the church, must have felt he needed the church, and this was the one church that he knew. While all this happened, I had already struck a deal that would exclude me from ever having to attend Victoria Temple, so I never saw Gabriel Soto there. Now, for some secret reason, Gabriel Soto was not ever coming back to church.

I flipped the pages of the phone book to get to my name, my house, and number where I lived and where my Aunt Teresa had died. I saw no blue and no green and no red.

I was an unmarked man.

"I have to visit with one of the elders this morning, Bert; otherwise, I would chat with you here in this cool blue room all day. I am going to call you this afternoon. I am going to call you at 1 p.m. and ask you three very important questions, and whatever you say, however you respond, I will have my markers on me, so I don't forget."

It was 8 a.m. when I shut the back door and started walking away from Victoria Temple, eating a blueberry cereal bar and feeling the sun make the city unbearably bright. I never drank when I wrote obits and usually celebrated the completion of getting an obit into *The Verger* by drinking to the dead and then staying put in my cold room for the day. My Aunt Teresa never drank, and I never wanted to drink when I was in front of her, so I just went back to my cold room to look at the funeral flowers that were sprayed so stiff they would look good for another week. I got up to lie down on the tiles of my kitchen, closed my eyes to see the dots you see when you come from bright and close your eyes in a darker place, and waited for the call.